REDEEMED AND ENLIGHTENED

DENNIS PAUL STRADFORD

SANCTUS SPIRITUS
PRESS

San Francisco

REDEEMED AND ENLIGHTENED

2014 Sanctus Spiritus Trade Paperback Edition

Published in the United States of America.

ISBN-10: 0692313958
ISBN-13: 978-0692313954

Library of Congress Control Number: 2014919169

www.DennisStradford.com

SANCTUS SPIRITUS
PRESS

San Francisco

Praise for Dennis Paul Stradford

"The romance and dark intrigue of the Roman Church is perfectly captured in the latest in Dennis Paul Stradford's "Redeemed" series, *Redeemed and Enlightened*. Set amidst the panoply of San Francisco society from the hilltop mansions of Pacific Heights to the colorful streets of the Mission District, the novel continues the saga of handsome young priest, Billy Fernandez, as he risks his faith and his vocation to follow the truth of his love."

Dick Smart
"Book Lovers" Lambda Literary

"*Redeemed and Enlightened*, like all of Stradford's books, pushes the reader to explore the grey area of human nature. The author creates complex, dynamic characters who face extraordinary challenges both in Stradford's richly created secular and religious worlds, and in their deepest often troubled selves."

James Warren Boyd
University of San Francisco

"It just gets better with each new volume! In *Redeemed and Enlightened*, Stradford's many fans as well as new readers will delight in the clerical capers and escapades on at least two levels: the amazing and bewildering – and oh so human – predicaments that people of faith can get into. But also, and on a deeper level: in the midst of delicious scandals, authentic lives of grace shine through."

David Kundtz
Author of *Coming To: A Biomythography*

"Anyone familiar with the history of Roman Catholic seminary life, knows that in the late 1960s and early1970s, there

Praise for Dennis Paul Stradford

were radical changes in its cult and culture, changes which mirrored the broader secular culture, but were rarely revealed. So if you want to know one real inside story about those years and beyond - in the seminary and out - and if you enjoy an intimate insight into lives not normally exposed, Stradford serves them both up with accuracy, an unflinching eye and, one of the book's significant accomplishments, a deep sense of the spiritual struggles of his characters.

"It's all here: sex, intrigue, politics, broken vows, fidelity, cover-ups, and finally faith - as well as the sordid and noble deeds of a handful of fascinating people who attempt to live it. This is a quick-moving story that resists the too common trait of many religion-based tales of over-describing and mistaking pomp for something interesting. It also gives the reader the feeling of being "allowed in" to private lives and intimate moments.

"I think it was C.S. Lewis who said that in his experience one is either strongly attracted to or strongly repelled by clerics, but rarely neutral toward them. Stradford provides plenty of both."

David, Amazon Review of *Blessed and Betrayed*

"This is a fascinating story of love, sex, lies and faith, all set in a Catholic seminary which values propriety, power and purpose. For Catholics, Protestants, Gays and Straights, this book is a challenging insight into the world of the evolving 20th Century Catholic church, and the struggles many in the Church face reconciling their sexuality with their presumed morality. The author writes from experience, and with passion. While enjoying a colorful and challenging story, I've also learned much about the complexity of faith, allegiance, deception, and redemption. Enjoy!"

Peter, Amazon Review of *Blessed and Betrayed*

To Guy Writers:
Bud, Jake, Chris, James, Gabriel and Martin
for their support, sharp critique and helpful
suggestions.

AUTHOR'S NOTE

Redeemed and Enlightened brings to a close the story of a 40 year journey that is both spiritual and lustily passionate, religious and gay, populated with saints and sinners who struggle to make sense of an ancient Catholic tradition and the evolving understanding of healthy human sexuality.

It is a saga of all too human desires for love, power, meaning and joy and the needs for stability, order and personal satisfaction among the rich, the poor, the addicted and the sacrosanct. I hope there is something for every reader to identify with, however uncomfortable that may be at times and that the story rings true to life.

~ Dennis Paul Stradford

REDEEMED
AND
ENLIGHTENED

1

The gentle brush of a soft lip was

so brief and so quick, yet it produced a deep, long lasting stir in his groin. Overwhelmed by an impulsive surge of erotic energy, he grabbed the back of the head that attempted to be elusive and pulled the mouth of those tender red lips deeper and deeper into his own, their tongues dancing a duel at once combative and caring. Not letting up on the energetic caress which grew increasing like a wrestle, Billy savored the taste of salty sweat as he licked the freshly shaved cheek. The sensation of stubble on his tongue increased his excitement and he was surprised to hear himself moan with desire.

He felt the need to admonish himself to quiet down, though he felt powerless to do so.

He grabbed the head of hair with both hands and felt his own head seized in the same manner. With a desperate rocking back and forth, he rolled and thrust his pelvis in ever increasing force. He yearned to look deep into those blue eyes but did not want to take even a second away from the sensation enveloping his tongue and mouth.

As they writhed in excitement, the sensation of a hard large cock pressing against his stomach led him only to want to surrender to its power, to give way to all his desires regardless of the consequences. Nothing mattered now but fulfillment. "Please fuck me, oh please, please fuck me," he begged between moans. He spread his legs apart, opening himself to the anticipated sensation of being filled with a strong warm dick pulsating against his prostate, driving him into ecstatic pleasure, helpless to resist, with only a desire to surrender. It would happen soon, very soon. He felt a growing urgency to have this sweet man inside him, to be joined in sweaty, wild bliss, when in the far reaches of his consciousness he felt the sensation of cum over his stomach and its stickiness to the sheets.

Slowly he opened his eyes to the faint light filtering in through the shaded window. He stared at the ceiling, then glanced over to the bright red numbers on his alarm clock, which read 6:18. Billy sighed.

"I've made another mess of the sheets, damn! Mrs. Garcia will surely say something this time," he half muttered to himself. Mrs. Garcia, the short and rotund housekeeper, had a special place in her heart for Father Billy Fernandez, though she was not adverse to admonishing him for leaving his dirty underwear lying on the floor of his bathroom or holding them up to the light for an inspection before throwing them into the wash hamper, which she did once a week.

Throwing the top sheet and blanket off his still sweating body, he threw his legs over the side of the bed and looked down to see his cock still large, though not fully erect, panting like a Thoroughbred just finished with a race, and the sight of a large quantity of cum sticking to the hair traveling from his navel down to a substantial dark curly bush. He jumped up and walked toward the shower. "Maybe if I jacked off more, this wouldn't happen." It was a sensible thought, but secretly he enjoyed these dreams a great deal. They were so much more real than the fantasies conjured up by looking at porn or remembering the look of a handsome man he had met during the day.

His dreams were guilt free pleasures that he had no control over, sort of a gift from God. They were guilt free, conflict free and disease free, with the only consequence being a minor embarrassment of stained sheets. Not his fault. Nothing to confess. Nothing to worry over. They were occurring more often too, at least twice a week lately.

It was too early to get up but too late to go back to sleep, so he sat pondering his next move. After resting five minutes with his eyes shut, he slowly rose and headed toward the bathroom and a hot shower. A thorough scrubbing with the new pine scented washing gel initiated a sensual feeling he liked more every day, both the feel on his skin and the aroma it gave. He began to get excited again, especially as he scrubbed his ass and the tender area between his cheeks. Closing his eyes he began to remember the scene of his dream and felt his cock was hardening again. Who was the handsome man he was so intent on devouring, whose passionate kisses tingled his whole body? Drifting back to the reverie of just moments ago he wanted to go back to bed, pull the sheets up and lose himself again in an erotic trance.

Like an unwelcome intruder, the thought of preparing for the 7:30 Mass nudged its way to the front of his consciousness and the obligations of his priestly life snuffed out what remained of his carnal desires. Rinsing off, his mind started listing the tasks of the day: Mass. A visit to the nursing home across the street to bring communion to forty or so Catholics in their last stages of dementia. Teach religion class at the school for third and fifth grades. Meet with the parent's committee preparing the eighth graders for confirmation. Maybe a quick sandwich. A hospital visit to Mrs. Rodriquez that he had promised last Sunday but had forgotten to do for the last three days. A meeting with the four new altar boys to instruct them on the funeral mass for Mr. Gonzales who died of cancer at 41 which was scheduled for 4 p.m. Then after the Funeral Mass, go to the cemetery in Colma for the burial. Attend the wake at the Gonzales' home to comfort his wife, five children, four brothers and their wives and his parents and grandmother who flew in from Mexico. Rush to Duggan's Mortuary for an 8:30 p.m. rosary for Mrs. Rosas who died four days ago at a more acceptable age of 81. And finally return to the rectory to put his feet up at 10 p.m., perhaps to watch a little TV. Yes, it would be normal Wednesday, 7:30 a.m. to 10 p.m., half spent speaking his native Spanish, the other half trying to improve his English. He had learned it young, going to high school just two miles away. Even though he barely had an accent, his subsequent eight years in Mexico and Rome had stilted his vocabulary and grammar usage and he was insecure about it.

Billy liked being a priest. He liked being busy and he like the feeling of being needed. It was two years since his move to San Francisco from Rome and he especially enjoyed being back in the U.S. His assignment to the Basilica of Mission Dolores, the original mission that founded San Francisco and the center of the Mission District, was a godsend as well. The Basilica, a large Church in the ornate Spanish baroque style, reminded Billy of his life in Mexico, yet it had the plush, rich interior of an American Church. Next to the Basilica was the original Mission Adobe Church of the Mexican Franciscan padres who first explored California and founded the city of San Francisco. Connecting to that history gave Billy comfort and helped him to feel not so alone.

The surrounding Mission District was now largely Latino, though there were Catholic Vietnamese and Cambodians, as well. A few Irish were rooted in their family homes in what had once upon a time been an almost exclusively Irish neighborhood. It was a lively place to live, with lots of single twenty-somethings, both gay and straight, interspersed with the many families that added a certain energy that was unique to the Mission. Mostly he felt welcomed and accepted, but occasionally there would be stares at his Roman Collar, stares that he couldn't tell if they were meant to be unfriendly or just the shock of surprise, as if someone had seen a ghost.

He lived in the rectory with Father Red Reilly, a 68-year-old priest of the old school. People who knew him for many years called him Red for his famously bright red hair of which there was not one single strand left. Every hair, on his balding head, his arms and hands, were completely white. To newcomers, the reason to call him Red was his reddish complexion due to the thousands of pulsating blood vessels on his nose, forehead and cheeks. Though he had been sober for nearly a decade thanks to AA, the years of heavy drinking showed on Red Reilly's face like battle scars. At five feet five inches, gauntly thin and bad teeth, he exuded a nervous energy that gave the impression of being jumpy. A slight twitch of his left eye added to the general sense that he was a nervous fellow. With a ready, crooked smile, one immediately sensed he was approachable and friendly. He was the favorite of the Irish still in the Mission and he got a great deal of solace from being their "old fashioned" priest. He was invited to every party, picnic, and gathering. His role was father of the community, esteemed by everyone, but he was humble in the role because of his battle with alcohol. The Latino community thought well of him because he stood up for them with immigration officials, the city health department and the police when it was necessary, though for the past two years their clear favorite and darling was their new priest Father Billy Fernandez.

Billy liked Red, but found it hard to get close to him. First, he was the Pastor and his direct superior, and though Red was always friendly, he had no problem giving Billy clear directions and instruction. Billy never felt like he was a peer of the pastor; he was the junior assistant and expected to stay in his place. Though Billy was drawn to older men, there was no attraction to Red or chemistry between them. He missed the close collaboration he had had with Father Filiberto in Rome, who was older than Red, yet made Billy feel an equal in all things.

In fact, in the two years he had been in San Francisco, Billy had not made any priestly friends. He stayed close to this mother, visiting her every Sunday evening for dinner, where after the meal they would watch Mexican soap operas until he returned to the rectory. His mother was adoring, loving, and pious; the center of her life was her only child, now a holy priest. Nearing sixty years old, Billy's mother had a group of old lady friends that kept her company, mostly from her "off the books" job at the vegetable stand on 19th Street. She and Billy had illegally entered the U.S. over twelve years ago when her husband had been killed in a feud among Mexican mafia chieftains. Billy had been discovered and deported just as he was finishing high school. Undetected by the INS, his mother

16

had been able to remain in San Francisco. The years of loneliness and worry had fueled her intense prayers to Our Lady of Guadalupe. She believed all of them had been answered in the most miraculous way by their current reunion. In the years between high school and his ordination, Billy had lived alone in a sophisticated and intellectual world that was way beyond his mother's experience, so that while he dearly loved her, she provided little companionship or real emotional support to him. In particular she had no clue as to his sexual orientation and desires. For that matter neither did Red Reilly or anyone else he had come to know in the parish.

Day in and day out, Billy worked exceedingly hard at being the best priest he could be, taking the few pointers Red gave him. The positive response from the many families he had come to know was an indication that he was doing a good job. The work was emotionally and physically exhausting and there never seemed to be an end to the demand for his time. He was supposed to have one day a week off, but found himself working those days as well because so many people were asking for him. Besides, he really didn't have anyone to spend the day with. Staying in his room alone made him very conscious of how lonely he was. The temptation of his sexual fantasies seemed the only way to fill the time. Billy had yet to find a confessor to whom he could unburden himself. The mounting weight of his sins began to increase over the months. He began to overly criticize his sermons or the way he was saying Mass. When he heard confessions, he would get short with the little old ladies who seemed to confess the most trivial of sins, the men who confessed the same infidelities over and over again or the teenagers who obsessed over impure thoughts and masturbation. Billy always wanted to excuse that, but the pious fifteen year old wanted to make it deadly serious. The only solution was to work harder, find some time to pray and be the priest that everyone expected and needed him to be.

As Billy was downing a quick cup of coffee after the morning mass, Red popped into the kitchen with a look of dread on his face.

"The new Archbishop is coming this Sunday to say the 10:30 mass. I just got a call from his secretary," Red said. "You need to get the altar boys up to snuff. This guy is a stickler for doing everything perfect in the liturgy. From what I hear through the grapevine, he loves pomp and circumstance and goes all out to show off his ecclesiastical regalia." Red arched his eyebrow. "He gets pretty upset if people make mistakes. You know all that stuff from your Roman training I'm sure, so I'm putting you in charge. We will both concelebrate with him, but I wish I could just disappear."

"Really? What is this guy like? I don't know anything about him," Billy replied.

"I don't either really. He came from Philadelphia. Has some connections with the Cardinal there. You will probably like him. He speaks Spanish pretty well and likes Latinos. Says they are the future of the Church. I'm sure the Pope likes that line. But he's death on the sex issues, birth control and abortion. He's a bit wacko on gay marriage. Sees the devil working overtime to destroy the family, which hasn't played that well here, as you might imagine." Red scratched his jaw. "Anyway, let's give him a good show at mass, send him on his way and hope we don't hear from him again for a few years." Red spit out in a fury, "Bishops are a real pain in the ass, always wanting to make sure everyone is following the rules, or at least the rules they think are important. He'll move on sooner or later. San Francisco is small time for a man with ambition, and I hear he has plenty of it."

Billy was taken aback by Red's dark fervor, a side of him he hadn't seen before.

"I'll do my best," Billy replied.

"Oh, and by the way. Be sure to always call him "Your Excellency." He dislikes the informality of being called Archbishop, much less by his name. Go tell," Red said, shaking his head.

Billy went to the sacristy an hour before the Sunday 10:30 Mass to make sure all the vestments were laid out just so. He had the three altar boys lined up, fully cassocked and ready when the Archbishop swept in at exactly 10:15.

Red made the introductions, "Your Excellency, this is Father Fernandez, my young assistant."

"Ah, Father, splendid to meet you. I heard you were ordained by our Holy Father himself, right after he was elected Pope. What an honor," the Archbishop said extending his hand in a way that made is easy for Billy to kiss his ring.

"Yes, your Excellency. It was a wonderful experience, one that I will never forget." Billy looked the Archbishop directly in the eye as he spoke. He noticed that he was being thoroughly appraised, in a way that reminded him of his first meeting with another prelate, Monsignor Munoz many years before. The warm and inviting look on the Archbishop's face reflected that he liked everything that he was seeing.

"Well, let's get ready for our celebration, shall we? Father Cody here is my secretary and will serve as Master of Ceremonies. He knows exactly the way I want the liturgy celebrated and will ensure we adhere to all the correct rubrics." The Archbishop motioned behind him to a short, middle-aged rotund priest who was carrying two large suitcases.

"Morning fathers," Father Cody said.

Father Cody laid out the suitcases on the floor and

opened each. The Archbishop stepped toward the counter where the mass vestments were laid out and took off his coat, unbuttoned his clerical "rabi" collar and placed them on the chair next to him. Underneath he had a heavily starched collarless white shirt, with French cuffs and gold cufflinks designed with a cross. He stood waiting as Father Cody pulled out a bishop's cassock with red piping on the sleeves and a row of buttons down the front. He held the cassock up for the Archbishop to place his arms into the sleeves. He then quickly ran to the front and, crouching down, began to button the row of buttons, which took a while since there were so many. Then Father Cody reached back into the suitcase for a large crucifix on a thick gold chain and gently placed it over the Archbishop's head and affixed the cross to a buttonhole in the middle of his chest.

All the while being dressed by Father Cody, the Archbishop looked slightly toward the ceiling with a smile on his face. He now moved toward the mirror on the wall and looked himself up and down, admiring what he saw, slightly adjusting the cross. He returned to the counter where Father Cody continued to dress him, first with the white *alb* and *cincture*. Father Cody then presented him with the priestly *stole*, which the Archbishop kissed. He bent his head so that it could be placed around his neck. After the *chasuble* was placed over his head, Father Cody reached into the suitcase for the *pallium*, which signified the wearer was a metropolitan archbishop, and placed it over his head. Two ornate episcopal gloves appeared and were fitted onto the Archbishop's hands. Finally, a red skullcap was placed on his head, and a large gold and white *miter* on top of that.

During the entire time this "dressing" was taking place, Billy, Red and the three altar boys stood at the back of the sacristy and watched in complete silence. Billy was brought back to his memories of Rome and the theatrics he had observed so many times for Cardinal Lucelli, his old boss and mentor. As he prepared for mass, Lucelli was attended to and treated like the royal prince that he was. It was all part of the medieval "romanitas" culture of the Catholic Church in the Vatican, but it rarely showed up in the hinterlands, like San Francisco. Obviously this new leader of the San Francisco Archdiocese was in love with all the pomp and splendor of medieval Rome, and he intended to live it out here in this most secular and liberal city in the twenty-first century.

The Archbishop turned around to face them, appearing quite a bit more imposing than his five foot six inch frame had originally presented. "Fathers, don't you think you should vest? Father Cody, my *crozier* please."

Father Cody hurriedly went to the suitcase and produced three pieces of an ornate brass crozier that he screwed together to create the long shepherd staff that all bishops use as they process toward the altar and bless the congregation. Father Cody quickly got into a black cassock and donned a white, ornate *surplus*.

Once all were vested, the Archbishop bent his head and recited a short prayer in Latin calling for the Holy Spirit to be present. He looked up and commanded, "Let us proceed with the grace of God."

The mass went off without any major faux pas, though the church was only half filled and the choir sang off key several times. The Archbishop's sermon was short and filled with pious platitudes, which got the standard response from a bored audience. A great number of babies cried and loud, restless children were told to sit still.

Billy observed how the Archbishop said Mass. Every

move was precise and intensely perfect. He held his hands up just so when saying the prayers, exactly even on each side of his body, all fingers pressed together. When he spoke the words of consecration, he breathed them out on the host in a way that appeared as if the Archbishop's breath was actually turning the bread into the body of Christ. When he gave communion, he did so in an authoritarian manner that seemed to challenge the worthiness of each recipient. Processing out of the Church, he held his head high as he gave blessings to the people, careful not to make eye contact with any of them.

As the celebrants returned to the sacristy, Father Cody proceeded to undress the Archbishop just as he had dressed him. Billy and Red waited to escort him to the rectory for a small lunch, clerics only. While the three priests had changed into their black clerical shirts, the Archbishop chose to stay in his episcopal cassock.

As they sat at the table, a bowl of soup and a platter of sandwiches had been laid out waiting for them, all in keeping with Red's simple style of living.

"A simple fare today Father? I was wondering, would it be possible to have some wine with lunch? It's a habit I picked up in Rome and like to keep," the Archbishop said, trying not to appear disappointed in the food.

Red went searching in the kitchen for a bottle of wine, which took a while as he and Billy did not drink at meals. In his absence, the Archbishop turned to Billy, smiling profusely. "So tell me Father, how is the Church faring in the Latino community here?"

"Well, I suppose, your Excellency. Many of the immigrants are very loyal to the Church and want to keep their customs, which often remind them of their homeland. When you say Latino, of course there are many different cultures under that name. Mexican, Salvadorian, Honduran, various South American cultures. It is not just one big group," Billy responded.

"This is true, but they all look to the Church for guidance and leadership. My experience has shown me that many of these simple families are deeply troubled by the diverse and secular lifestyles of Americans and are shocked, scandalized and troubled by what they find here. They fear their children will be corrupted by the pop culture of "anything goes" and lose their faith, or worse."

Billy watched the Archbishop as he got more and more animated when talking about the evils of society. Small veins popped out at the side of his temples and his white complexion reddened. He obviously felt deeply about what he was speaking, but the emotion that Billy sensed the most from him was anger. He was angry at the temptations of the world and how it led people astray. When angry, Billy felt the man's power come alive.

Earlier Billy had thought the Archbishop was a pretty mild-mannered man, not quite sure of himself around others, relying on his position to give him confidence. He was good looking, trim though short, with a nice smile, and was perhaps in his late 50's though he looked younger. He was very well groomed, Billy noticed, and well-manicured. His nails were perfectly shaped and shiny. His blue eyes were clear and hinted at intelligence, but when getting emotional, Billy noticed that his eyes darted back and forth at a frantic pace. Having been around many Cardinals of the Curia and having met the Pope, he was not intimidated by this Archbishop in the least. Billy felt good about that and was pleased with how he presented himself. The Archbishop noticed his confidence as well.

Red returned with a bottle of wine, opened it and

poured a glass for the Archbishop and Father Cody. He motioned to Billy, who declined. After taking a rather large gulp, the Archbishop appeared to calm down a bit and began asking Red the usual questions about the parish. How many children were in the school? What is the attendance at Mass? What's the financial situation? The answers were short and the comments by the Archbishop perfunctory.

As the small lunch was ending, the Archbishop, pouring a second glass of wine for himself (it was the first time Billy had seen him do anything for himself), turned to Billy. "I'd like to hear your thoughts, Father Fernandez, about what you think the Archdiocese should do to further meet the needs of the Latino community in San Francisco?"

"Well, your Excellency, I have some ideas, but I would rather say I don't know. Because I don't. What I would suggest is that a task force be set up to hold small meetings with the various segments of the community and ask them what they would like to see from the Church. What areas of their life would they like to see the Church play a stronger role in? I'm sure immigration assistance, help with medical needs, programs for young people during the long summer break would come up. But there might be more and we should listen directly to the community to find what they feel are their pressing needs," Billy replied straightforwardly.

"Yes, I like that idea. I was thinking along similar lines. I want to hear more, Father. Perhaps you and Father Cody can set up a time for you to visit me and you can help us develop a plan," the Archbishop relied. He stood up and finished the last of his wine. "Fathers, it has been wonderful, but I must depart for my next meeting. Thank you for lunch. Your staff did you credit this morning Father Reilly."

Shaking hands and receiving the final kiss of the ring,

the Archbishop departed.

Red turned to Billy. "He likes you. My God, be careful."

2

Monsignor Al Pevehaus was
lounging around his penthouse apartment near the Via Ve-
nato in Rome in his underwear, stepping over discarded news-
papers, clothes and trash that he had difficulty summoning
the energy to clean up. The summer heat, now that it was July,
was getting to the unbearable point, even with his air condi-
tioning, which was really only designed for a bedroom. Wandering from room to room, he was feeling more lost than at
any point in his life. For the last month, he spent many hours
watching movies on his DVD player, sometimes five or six a
day. Occasionally he read trashy gay mysteries and sometimes
masturbated to his worn out porn collection. He like to think
they were classics, but in fact, they were just familiar and a
few scenes sometimes sparked euphoric memories of Jim or
Billy, the men he had truly loved in his life. He'd sworn off
going out to clubs and hiring rent boys because he had vowed

to reform his life and regain his connection to God through working with Brother Antonius, his only real friend in Rome and his spiritual guide. With Brother Antonius, he had recovered some peace and serenity. He drank less, though still regularly, and needed sleeping pills only on certain difficult nights. He had abstained from all other drugs as well. He had thought he was on a path, a road to recovering some happiness in his life.

It had been a restful and reasonably contented year since his Vatican career had come crashing down with his forced resignation at the Vatican Bank. Al Pevehaus had been disgraced, even though he had shown great courage to reveal the Mexican Drug Cartel's plot to control the Vatican Bank, a scandal that brought down the Pope's own secretary, Monsignor Munoz. But his prospects for a future at the Vatican were over. He had supposedly "retired" to the Franciscan Retreat House at St. Francesco di Ripa Grande, but in fact, he only spend three or four days a week there helping Brother Antonius in the garden. In the beginning, that had been enough to enjoy his life, regain some emotional stability and put away many of his self-destructive habits.

Suddenly, a month ago, Brother Antonius had been transferred to another Franciscan house in Italy. Not only did Al lose his mentor, friend and spiritual guide, but the focused work in the garden had come to an end. Al was deeply shaken by this change. He felt as if his legs had been pulled out from underneath him. His loneliness felt more than he could bear. The man who had sparked a new self-respect within him, who was his emotional guidepost by which he could reflect on the meaning of his life and who he felt had unfailingly loved him, was gone in a flash. As the last month passed he increasingly felt there was no reason to go on living.

Looking at himself in the mirror that morning, he saw how age and the stress of his past secret and rather debauched life had taken its toll. The deep lines under his eyes, the splotchy cheeks and veiny nose showed the years of too much alcohol. The potbelly, already present when he came to the Vatican, had been substantially increased by the rich Roman pasta. Finally, he found the oblong balding forehead, crowned by stringy gray hair, to be extremely unattractive. Everything in the mirror told him he was not just well past his prime but on the downhill slide to death. Ironically, at sixty-four, he still had too much energy to really retire. When he first retired, he enjoyed his ample free time but, over the last several months, he had become more and more restless. He had far too much time on his hands. His energy compounded the free time to make every waking moment vacillate between anxiety and dark depression. With Brother Antonius gone, every day had become a burden that weighed more and more heavily upon him.

He had been too depressed to even check his mail from the lobby downstairs. As he was out of food, today he would have to go out, and he committed himself to look at the mail. It had been two weeks but he was sure there would be only bills. Even though he had plenty of money to pay them, they demoralized him.

Near mid-day, he finally dressed in khaki shorts, tennis shoes and a faded orange tank top. He took his shopping bag and went outside, the first time in three days. He greeted a couple of shopkeepers he knew, one of whom insisted on calling him Padre. He bought the usual fare of pasta, cheese, a few vegetables and six bottles of his favorite Chianti. Returning home, he almost forgot to check the mail again, but he glanced and could see the metal box was stuffed with envelopes. He quickly grabbed them, continued upstairs and threw them on the table as he put the groceries away. Afterwards he stared at the bills for a few moments, trying to get up the energy to open them. In the middle of the stack was a surprise, a letter from the Archdiocese of San Francisco.

> *Dear Monsignor Pevehaus,*
> *I am writing on behalf of his Excellency, Archbishop Sylvester Peterson, who sends his greetings. He understands you are currently without assignment in Rome. He wonders if you would consider returning to your home diocese and take up a position here. He has reviewed your resume and would welcome a meeting to discuss opportunities that are developing in San Francisco. Please reply at your earliest convenience.*
> *Sincerely yours in Christ,*
> *Father William Cody, Secretary to the Archbishop*

Al was astounded. He was so out of the loop that he didn't even know there was a new Archbishop in San Francisco. His predecessor, Archbishop O'Brien had made it clear to Al a couple of years previous that he was not wanted back in San Francisco and that he should stay in Rome. Quickly Al sat at his computer and began researching his new ordinary. He was young, only fifty-seven and a canon lawyer. This did not surprise him, as 90 percent of bishops appointed over the last decade were Church lawyers. He originally came from the Philadelphia Archdiocese and had been a bishop of Allentown, Pennsylvania before his appointment to San Francisco. That meant his powerbase was East Coast, most likely the Cardinal Archbishop of Philadelphia. It also meant he would know nothing of San Francisco, its politics or society, areas in which Al had been an expert. "*Perhaps there is a future for me in San Francisco*," he thought.

Al looked at the letter. It had arrived over a week ago and was dated back nearly three weeks. Italian mail was still the slowest in the world. He decided to call directly to Father Cody, a priest he knew a bit, but would have to wait until the early evening, which would be morning in California. His whole day brightened up. He was ready to leave Rome. There was nothing to keep him there any longer and he missed San Francisco. He began to fantasize about returning as the con-quering hero, sweeping in to help the new Archbishop estab-lish a powerbase among the wealthy and well-connected of Pacific Heights. He could bring his considerable organization-al skills to fix the problems left over from the previous regime. He could start over. It was a milieu that he knew and where he had had great success in the past.

The thought of seeing Billy Fernandez again also found its way to the front of his consciousness. He wondered how he was doing as a parish priest. He also wondered what their relationship might be like if he returned. Billy was too old at twenty-seven to be really attractive to Al, although he was certainly very handsome. But he also deeply loved Billy in a certain way, a way that former lovers have with each other, even though the relationship is over. He had some wonder-ful memories of their time together when Billy was in high school, trips they had taken, dinners exploring new food and the wonderful times in bed. He felt they had worked out a new relationship in Rome, even though it was complicated by the stress of dealing with Billy's uncle and the attempts by the Mexican drug cartel to manipulate Al into compromising the Vatican Bank. He was eager to see Billy and did not feel a great deal of stress that their relationship might present an awkwardness or a threat to him.

A week later, Al checked into the Fairmont Hotel on Nob Hill. The call to Father Cody had gone very well and an appointment with the Archbishop had been set almost immediately. His appointment was for 4 p.m. Al visited the spa in the morning, worked out a little, got a haircut, a manicure and spent some time in the steam room to improve his complexion. He wore his best Italian suit, rabi, collar and diamond cufflinks. He wanted to look every inch the Roman monsignor.

Father Cody announced him, "Monsignor Pevehaus, your Excellency."

The Archbishop came from around his desk with his hand outstretched. Picking up the clue by how high the hand was held, Al knelt and kissed the Archbishop's ring as if it were a relic. Standing, he bowed slightly. "Your Excellency, my congratulations on your appointment to this great and famous see."

"Why thank you Monsignor. It has been over six months and I am beginning to get the lay of the land. It was good of you to fly over from the Eternal City on such short notice to visit with me," the Archbishop said, motioning to Al to sit on the sofa at the side of the office. The Archbishop sat opposite him in a chair.

"I was gratified to receive the letter from Father Cody that there might be an opportunity here in San Francisco and that you were interested in meeting me," Al said.

"Yes, yes. I understand that you had quite a good track record here in San Francisco. Father Cody tells me you did your excellent work with Catholic Charities, turning around the financial situation at Serra High School and that you built two new Churches as well. I gather there were some political difficulties with the planning commission on the new Cathedral project. Those things do happen."

"Well, your Excellency, sometimes our failures teach us the most. I learned from my mistakes and I hope I am a wiser and more astute man today," Al replied, trying to balance a sense of humility with confidence.

"Tell me, what of your experience at the Holy See?"

"Well, I spent several years working for Cardinal Lucelli at the Pontifical Commission on the Pastoral Care of Migrants and Itinerant Peoples. That job gave me a unique perspective on the Church's mission to the many communities of migrants around the world and how to better serve them. I most recently occupied a position as secretary to the Board of Cardinals at the Vatican Bank, but frankly that position did not suit me well, and having a few health problems, I resigned about a year ago and have been taking a much needed rest," Al spoke positively, trying to put the best shine onto the dull career he had had in Rome.

"And are you fully restored to health now?" the Archbishop asked.

"I think so, your Excellency."

"Good. I think you may be able to help us here in San Francisco again, if that be your wish." The Archbishop leaned back in his chair and looked toward the ceiling. "For various reasons, I think I need a man with good contacts in the wealthier set of Catholics here, and I understand you had many friends and contacts in that group." Leaning forward he looked at Al with a furrow in his brow. "To be blunt, I find myself not very welcome in those circles, primarily because of my strong conviction and public position on the abomination of Gay Marriage, which many in that rich crowd support. For the life of me I do not understand how they believe they can be good Catholics and support such a wicked thing, but many do. If I could ban them from communion I would. I would make sure their children did not get into those choice schools they so covet too. However, the Latino community here completely supports me. But that snobby, well-heeled and wildly liberal clique are keeping me at a distance, and most importantly have cut donations to the some very important causes here in the Archdiocese. Our fund raising efforts have dropped significantly."

Al noticed the bulging veins in his forehead and the darting eyes as the Archbishop spoke, his rage almost turning into a rant. "Well, your Excellency, I know many of these people about which you speak. Yes, they may have liberal views, but they also have their own reasons to stay in the good graces of the Church, and can be appealed to on several levels. I am sure that I could accomplish your goals if I had some time to work with them. Are you thinking of another capital campaign?" Al asked.

"Yes and no. I want to raise a significant amount of money, but not to build buildings. I would like to create a fund to do more outreach to the Latino immigrant community. The demographics of San Francisco and California in general show that the future of the Church is with the Latino community and we must focus our efforts on keeping them in the Catholic fold and supporting their needs. They are the future of the Church here."

"Excellent idea your Excellency." Al pushed himself to sound very excited and confident. "I'm sure that idea will resonate with the Pacific Heights crowd, and I know exactly how to present it."

"Good. Then you will return. I will appoint you a special Vicar, reporting to me. You can live at the cathedral rectory, I think you lived there once before. I think you can even have your old room suite back." The Archbishop rose and presented his hand, which Al dutifully kissed once again. "How long will it take you to pack up in Rome?"

"No more than two weeks. It's starting to get hot in Rome, so the sooner I get back to the San Francisco fog the better."

"*That was short and sweet,*" Al thought happily as he walked down the street from the chancellery office. He reflected on the man he had just met. Their time together was too brief to take much measure of him, but there were certain impressions he wanted to consider and remember. The first was that the Archbishop was short, an unchangeable fact of life. Al had found that it produced a bit of a Napoleon complex, a strong need to be recognized as powerful, in ambitious men in the Church. This man seemed to rely heavily on his hierarchical position to assert his power. He recollected how much the Archbishop seemed to enjoy having his ring kissed. Secondly, he was intelligent, articulate, cool and very precise in his conversation. However, when he got emotional on a subject, such as Gay Marriage, he seemed to spit his words out with venom. Al had seen that behavior before as well, especially among a couple of Cardinals in Rome. It usually meant that there was a deep emotional conflict about whatever issue caused the heightened emotion. Al had picked up nothing on his "gaydar" but that didn't mean there wasn't a raging conflict going on within the man about his sexual feelings. Finally, Al thought the Archbishop a handsome man, with attractive and piercing blue eyes, what appeared to be a nice tan, a thinning head of hair but an expensive haircut and very well-manicured hands. He was dressed in an expensive suit without a wrinkle to be seen. Yes, Al thought, this Archbishop was not so different from men he had known before, especially at the Vatican. He was the consummate professional churchman, rich and polished, but also driven, both by ambition and his demons. Al would have to be very careful, but he thought he knew his man.

3

Billy appreciated Red's warning,
but he was only too aware of the Archbishop's interest in him
and that it wasn't all about reaching out to the Latino community. He had enough experience with priests like Al Pevehaus and Pedro Munoz to know full well that pious and
seemingly innocent intentions can mask a not so subtle sexual
attraction that clerics pretend is not there. Billy reflected that
sometimes it was a curse to be thought so good looking, that
some people's motivations seem to get so mixed up. With the
Archbishop, he had decided to play it very cool. He would
pose as someone naïve, unsophisticated and extremely humble, a persona he had practiced and learned well in Rome.
He would not call the chancellery office. He would assume
that the Archbishop was just being "nice" and far too busy
to bother with a lowly, young priest. Maybe the Archbishop
would forget about his request.

However, it did not take three days before Father Cody called the rectory asking Billy to call back and set an appointment. Knowing there was no way to avoid the meeting, Billy scheduled for a week later, citing his extreme busyness. He would go, play the role of an overworked and devoted priest, speak as little as possible and make sure he didn't volunteer for anything.

As he stepped into the Archbishop's office after being formally announced by Father Cody, he walked straight to the Archbishop, kissed his ring and searched for a place to sit. He moved to the couch at the far end of the office, sat down and looked up to the Archbishop staring at him with some bewilderment. Walking over to the chair opposite the couch, the prelate sat down.

"You are a very confident young man. I like that. It is a prized quality for Church leadership," the Archbishop smiled with a complementary look.

Billy appreciated that most young priests would be quite nervous and intimidated meeting with their bishop, but he had met with so many Cardinals in Rome, and even spent some time with the Pope, that a mere Archbishop was not very impressive to him.

"Thank you, your Excellency. I hope you don't take my manner as in any way disrespectful," Billy answered earnestly.

"No of course not. Thank you for taking the time out of your busy schedule to come visit me," the Archbishop replied graciously. "I want to follow up on the discussion we had at the rectory a couple of weeks ago. I was interested in your approach to surveying the Latino community on ways the Church might minister more effectively to them. I want to make an increased concentration on Latinos a major focus of my time here in San Francisco, one of my legacies as it were."

Billy thought that statement had an odd ring to it, first because it was clear Archbishop Sylvester Peterson did not plan to be in San Francisco for very many years; he would be promoted long before retirement or death. Secondly, the man was already thinking about his legacy when he had only been in his position for less than six months.

"I am grateful to hear that you have such a big interest for Latinos. Many are poor and in need of a great deal of hope as they struggle with living here, and I think their faith sustains them through very difficult times. That the Church should pay attention to them is important," Billy answered, now feeling that he was struggling with his English. The Archbishop switched to Spanish.

"Si, Si. Es muy importante por sus almas, especialmente."

Billy was impressed with the Archbishop's precise pronunciation and his obvious confidence in speaking, but he wanted to speak in English to make sure there were no misunderstandings, "Excellency, tell me how can I help?"

"Well, here is my idea. I want to develop a strategic plan for dramatically improving the Church's support and outreach to the Latino community. I want to take that plan to the wealthy of our diocese and raise a substantial amount of money to fund its execution. I would like you to lead the effort to develop the plan. I have another priest in mind to work on raising the money. He has expert contacts and is very good at getting people to write big checks." The Archbishop continued, "Perhaps you may know him. He recently has been in Rome as well. His name is Monsignor Allen Pevehaus."

Billy tried very hard to avoid showing his shock upon

hearing that name. He was unable to hide it altogether.

"It looks as though you have heard of him," the Archbishop nodded and smiled.

"Oh yes. I knew him through Cardinal Lucelli for whom I worked before I was assigned here. We have met on several occasions," Billy answered as calmly as he could.

"Well wonderful, then you two can start working together on this project sooner rather than later."

"Honestly, your Excellency, I do not know how I could find time to spend much effort on this survey right now. I am so busy with the work in the Parish, there are so many people in need and as the only native Spanish speaker, I am always running to the hospital, doing funerals and so many other things. I really spend every day running from one thing to another. I have no spare time," Billy said, hoping not to sound too desperate. "Besides, I have never done a survey. I thought it was a good idea, but I do not know how to do it. Shouldn't you find someone more expert than I?"

The Archbishop waved his hand dismissively. "Now Father, you are thinking shortsightedly. This project could have a big impact on the very people you are trying to serve and must take a priority. As for the survey, yes of course we can get experts involved to design it and ensure that it is well done. But you have a couple of unique traits that make you the perfect person to work on this project. First, since you come from Mexico, but have been trained in Rome, you have enormous credibility and trust within the Latino community. I have done some checking, and you are very highly thought of throughout the whole city among Latinos. With you introducing this survey to your people, I believe we will get a very high participation and honest feedback. You can help insure its accuracy and authenticity. Secondly, your intelligence, poise and good looks, I might add, will play very well in Pacific Heights, Nob Hill and Sea Cliff. Having you to present the strategic plan will be important in convincing our wealthy Catholics to open their pocketbooks to make large and significant donations. Father, I am convinced you are the right man for this job. Don't disappoint me."

Billy sat back, rather deflated. He was trapped and beginning to panic, not just to have to take on this new, unfamiliar work, but to have to spend time with Al Pevehaus, which could open up all kinds of issues he didn't want to face. "I'm not sure Father Reilly will be in favor of this, I mean, he needs me desperately to help him." Billy added in a last desperate attempt to forestall the inevitable, "We are both very overworked."

"I'll see what I can do to get Father Reilly some help," said the Archbishop with a stern, insistent look. "But I'm sure that if he knows it is his Archbishop's wish, he will cooperate completely." The smile was now gone from his face.

"Very well, your Excellency. Of course, I will leave it up to you and be happy to help." Billy knew there was no way out except to be blatantly disobedient, which would violate his priestly vows.

"Good. Leave everything to me." Standing, he lifted Billy up by the arm and put his hand on his shoulder. "I will contact you next week after I have organized a meeting with some people who can help with the survey. I will speak with Father Reilly directly and find a priest who can help out with Masses. This project is going to be a great success. Trust me." He was all smiles. Leaving his hand on Billy's shoulder a little too long and squeezing his muscle, the Archbishop looked almost lovingly at him.

Billy shifted a bit to show his discomfort, but the Archbishop was slow to take the hint and kept his hand still longer, forcing Billy to begin to walk toward the door.

"God Bless you."

Billy stopped, not knowing whether to bless him or how to respond. "Thank you your Excellency."

Heading back to Mission Dolores, Billy decided he needed to take a long walk. He headed toward Valencia Street, which was usually filled with the widest variety of Mission District residents. Walking among them somehow made him feel normal, like he was a regular person, not a rarified cleric who was now the new favorite of the Archbishop. He had a place in mind he wanted to visit and a person he wanted to talk with.

The New Hope Recovery House was just past 27th and Valencia in a narrow alleyway. In a rundown small apartment house, the center had a fifteen-bed detox center for alcoholics and drug addicts but also featured a daily schedule of "spirit centered" activities that promoted wellness for the whole person. These included poetry writing, yoga, furniture repair, movie discussions, cooking lessons, painting classes and the usual Twelve Step meetings morning and night. Sister Jane Matthews, a tough 60ish nun of the Social Services Sister, ran New Hope. She supervised a staff of over forty volunteers who freely put their time into helping the most desperate of the neighborhood. Billy had heard of the center several months ago from one of the sober "graduates" at the funeral of a not so successful resident. He was intrigued enough to stop in for a visit. Since then he had referred two clients to Sister Jane's care and in the process had enjoyed a couple of good but short conversations with her.

Billy needed to talk with someone he could trust. As he walked down the busy street, Sister Jane was the only face that came to mind. It was nearing 11 a.m. and he wondered if she was too busy to take a few minutes to speak with him. He walked through the front door of the center to discover a half dozen people lying on the floor, which alarmed him, but soon realized it was only a yoga session. He asked if Sister Jane was around.

"Sure, she's up on the second floor, in the bathroom," was the reply from a large black woman who he supposed was the instructor.

Billy said slightly embarrassed, "Oh, Okay. I'll wait."

"No, don't worry, she's cleaning. Go ahead, I'm sure she'd like the company."

Billy stepped carefully around the bodies on the floor and went up the staircase in the back corner. Walking down the corridor he heard the sound of a shower running at the end of the hallway. He stood outside the door.

"Sister Jane, are you in there?"

The nun poked her head out the door. She was wearing bright yellow rubber gloves that went all the way to her elbows and held a scrub brush in her hand. "Oh hello Father, what brings you down our way?"

"Oh Sister, sorry to interrupt. I was wondering if you have a few moments to talk," Billy replied, unable to stop staring at the gloves.

"Sure, but let me finish up quickly. This is the only time of day I can get in here and really clean this place. Give me five minutes. I'll see you downstairs," she replied, ducking back into the bathroom, resuming her work. "Oh, and hand me that mop in the hallway there."

Billy picked up the mop and went inside to hand it to her but immediately felt guilty that he should be offering to help. "Do you need a hand?"

"No, no. I'm almost finished. I've got my routine. Help will only slow me down!"

Billy walked downstairs and waited by the small office near the front door.

Ten minutes later, Sister Jane burst through the door. "So, how nice to see you again. How is life treating you, Father?"

Sister Jane was a fit, five foot five bundle of energy. She wore her full head of white hair short, in almost a crew cut, dressed in jeans and tennis shoes. She always sported a pretty white blouse with a gold crucifix around her neck that was large enough to draw your attention. She certainly did not look like a traditional nun, but somehow she also gave the immediate impression that she was a very religious person. Her steely blue eyes showed intelligence. Her ready smile and the surrounding lines of her cheeks offered a warmth that made one feel that the woman cared and was really focused on you and you alone.

"Well, Sister, life is full of surprises I guess. I've just come from a meeting with the Archbishop and I would like a chance to speak with you about it, if you have some time," Billy said, looking a little sheepish

"Oh. Him. Well." She looked around to see who was at the center. "It looks like we have enough staff right now. I'd love to take a break. Let's go for a walk. There's a park a few blocks from here, maybe we can find some grass to sit on."

As they walked down the street, she asked about Father Reilly and made a passing "hello" to an old lady pushing a shopping cart and a teenage Latino who was wearing the tough guy's low hanging baggy shorts and an oversized jersey. A long silver chain drooped from his belt.

They found a place to sit on the grass under a large bay

tree in the corner of the small park.

"So what does his highness want with you, Father? Or shouldn't I be so blunt in asking?" Sister Jane stared directly at Billy with a dimpled smile on her face.

"Oh please do!" he replied, grateful to get right to it. "A few weeks ago the Archbishop came to Mission Dolores to say Mass. At the small lunch afterward, he asked me some questions about the needs of the Latino community in the Mission, and what I thought were the important issues. Well, I didn't know how to answer him, so I told him I didn't know, but that I thought it would be a good idea to conduct a survey and find out directly what people thought. I should have kept my mouth shut, because he thought that I had a very good idea. He asked me come down to his office to discuss it. I tried to ignore that request, but his secretary called and insisted. We met this morning. He is taking my idea and making it a big project and he wants me to work with him on it, to be the person who introduces it to the community and organizes people to give their response."

"Well, it sounds like a good idea. Plus, this could be a big boost to your career. Most young priests would jump at the chance to get this kind of exposure. So what's the problem?"

"The problem is that I had my fill of exposure in Rome. My ambitions are to be a simple priest, as hidden from the hierarchy as I can be," Billy answered with a sigh. "And this guy makes me nervous."

"Oh, and why is that? I'm sorry, but you know I don't beat around the bush."

"Ugh, well, I don't know," Billy said, stalling for time, trying to figure out how honest to be with Sister Jane. "I guess it's that he's pompous, pretentious and reminds me too much of the ambitious guys I saw at the Vatican. It's just something I don't want to be around."

"Well, I can relate to that. I don't know the man myself, but from what I've heard and seen, he's not my cup of tea either. Are you sure there isn't something else?" she asked.

Billy waited a few moments. "I don't like the way he looks at me."

"Hmm. Like he's being just a little too friendly? That he's picking you for this job because he likes looking at you? You are very handsome you know," Jane said with a friendly smile on her face.

"Yes, I suppose. But I have a sensitivity to the way some prelates look at handsome young priests, and I worry about what expectations might develop, maybe certain fantasies, if you know what I mean."

"Yes. Yes, I think I do." Sister Jane sat for a moment, looking out over the grassy park. "So, how can I help?"

"Sister, since I've arrived here in San Francisco I haven't really found a spiritual director or confessor. In Rome, I came to know a truly holy priest who I could trust and who I could talk to, especially when I was confused or frightened. Believe me there was some frightening things going on the last year I was in Rome. I could never have survived without him. Well, I'm starting to feel like I really need someone to talk with, and you are the only person I have met that I think I can trust."

"Really?" Jane smiled and looked warmly at Billy. "I'm honored, and a bit taken aback. I'm not a priest, at least not yet, so I can't absolve you of your sins. But I can listen and give you feedback. If that is what you need, I think I can do that."

"Yes, that is what I need right now. But can we treat these conversations as if they were under the seal of confession? I mean, completely confidential?"

"Yes. I promise you that. And I promise not to hold anything back. What you hear will be my honest opinion," she said with a small grin and an imploring look in her eyes. "But I am only human too, so some times I can be wrong."

"Okay. I understand."

"So why does the Archbishop's little job for you have you so concerned? With your experience in Rome, you certainly know who to handle a prelate's wandering eye," she asked Billy, as he stared down at the ground.

"You are right, I can handle that issue. It wouldn't take much of a comment to back him off, especially given his feelings about homosexuals and the "gay agenda.'" He looked up at her, then paused a few moments. "The problem is that the Archbishop has brought a priest from Rome, whom I know, who is also going to be on this task force with me. We go way back. I mean way back."

"You want to tell me about it?"

Billy sighed deeply. "Alright. I knew this priest when I was in high school here in San Francisco. We grew very close. It's a long story, but eventually he came to see me as a threat and had me deported since at the time I was actually here illegally. It was a terrible shock, very traumatic. Eventually though, life back in Mexico turned out OK. I went to college. But I never got over this priest. I hated him and I loved him. And I wanted to be just like him. I mean I admired him so much." Billy paused to take a breath. "So I went to the seminary and managed to get an appointment to the Mexican seminary in Rome so I could be close to him, as I had heard that he had been transferred to the Vatican. So, we eventually met up in Rome and I found that he really didn't want me because I was too old for him, and I got over my obsession about him. At least, I think I have. But now that he is back and we are going to be working together, I'm worried maybe neither of us is really over each other. I just don't know. It could get very complicated."

"Is it fair to assume you had a sexual affair with this man when you were in high school?" Jane asked gently.

"Yes."

"Are you gay? Or did he manipulate you into going to bed with him?"

"Yes, I'm sure I'm gay, but since I went to the seminary I have been celibate," he answered, trying not to sound defensive.

"Good. Well, that makes two of us," Jane gave a chuckle.

"Really?" Billy looked shocked.

"What, you don't think nuns have a sexuality? We can't be gay too?"

"No, no. I just hadn't thought of it. Sorry, small-minded of me, I know," he answered sheepishly.

"That's OK. I don't make a big thing about it, but I'm not dishonest about it either. I've got nothing to hide. Jesus had no opinion about this issue, I mean, maybe he did, but there is nothing in the scripture about it. What He said really mattered was what we did for the poor and the needy and that we always forgive each other. But getting back to you and this priest, I think you need to pray for clarity about what kind of a relationship you want with him. I realize you may be feeling ambivalent and confused, but pray for clarity. Do you have a journal?"

"No."

"Well, get a notebook and start one. I find it is the best place to pray. Write and pray at the same time. Let the pen be guided by the Lord. He will tell you what you need to know. And pray for the willingness to follow His direction. If you are clear about what you want and what God wants for you, you can be clear with this priest, and you will be able to handle him, as well as you can handle the Archbishop. None of these people have power over you. With God on your side, you are safe and invincible."

"Thank you Sister." Billy patted her hand.

"You are welcome. I look forward to sharing this spiritual journey with you. God puts all of these challenges in our life for a reason, so that we may grow and progress. You are a good man, Father Billy. Call me any time and don't hesitate to come by regularly so we can talk."

They stood and began walking back to the center.

"You know, I have a story not that different from yours. I had a wonderful love affair with a nun in college. She opened my world in a way that still affects me. It lasted for over five years and I am so grateful for it." Jane spoke in a reverential tone.

"Do you still see her?" Billy asked.

"No, she passed away nearly twenty years ago. She is certainly with the Lord now, and I feel her prayers for me every day. She was a lovely women, a saint in her way with the sick and poor. I still miss her."

4

Pinky Lee put the finishing touches
on the exquisitely set table in the solarium and lit the fresh
candles. Even though it was to be a small, intimate dinner
party of only three—the master, the lady and their old friend
Monsignor Pevehaus, everything would still need to be perfectly elegant and richly stated but not ostentatious. Pinky
was the perfect major domo for such an affair. He could serve
the food almost invisibly, pour the wine just when the thought
entered a guest's mind and move about the table so quietly
there was not a sound. Fostering the feeling of intimate confidentiality, Pinky would ensure that nothing could interrupt
or interfere with the conversational flow. No one would speak
to him during the dinner nor would he say a word until, over
coffee, the master would simply say "Thank You, Pinky. That
was a lovely meal." This was his cue to disappear. Pinky prid-
ed himself on being the perfect Chinese houseboy.

Of course his name was not Pinky Lee. He was born Sung Lam Lee, but the master, John O'Malley Williams, had named him "Pinky" when he was first hired over twenty years ago. The master felt uncomfortable calling him "Sung Lam" and so gave him the first name that entered his head, a children's television star of the 1950's called Pinky Lee, an outrageously sissified clown who had mysterious disappeared from TV at the height of his popularity. He had been young John's favorite.

The Williams mansion at 2800 Pacific Street was one of many stately homes in the preferred area of Pacific Heights that was home to the very wealthy of San Francisco, particularly those who had inherited their wealth. It was the neighborhood of the very best of society, the place where those who sat on the Symphony board, the Opera board or the Modern Museum board could easily gather at each other's homes for the many gala fund raising events held all year long to keep the arts well-funded. It reinforced their elite status as the cultural movers and shakers of the city. Occasionally they would invite a nouveau riche venture capitalist that had recently cashed out of his high tech start up for several hundred million dollars or paid cash for a $35 million house on one of the select streets. Those folks were never really part of the "Pac Heights" crowd. For one thing, the newcomers had real names, like Bob or Dave or Kathy; the old money crowd had nicknames for each other like "Patsy" or "Spanky" or "Dotsy." When someone of the old money crowd was introduced to a newcomer, a phrase was always included to designate status, something like "and you know his mother was a Spreckles." The only iron clad rule for this haute society was that no matter what their behavior was, nothing was ever to appear in the newspaper or to be a cause for a television documentary. Their world was to always remain insular and private.

John O'Malley Williams had lived all of his fifty-five years in San Francisco, graduating from St. Ignatius High School and the University of San Francisco Law School. He had established himself as an estate-planning lawyer with Tobin and Tobin, the oldest law firm in the city. He was part of the Catholic elect in the city and was proud of the "O'Malley" middle name. His great, great grandfather, an Irish settler in the Gold Rush days of San Francisco, had done very well in the mines and had managed to hang on to his winnings. It was the O'Malley name that had given rise to the nickname of "Paddy." Paddy had married Rebecca Sullivan directly after college. "Becca," as she was called, had been a student at Lone Mountain College, the exclusive women's school run by the Madams of the Sacred Heart directly across the street from the University of San Francisco. The Sullivans were from lower Pacific Heights, an adjacent neighborhood down the hill towards the bay, but they were certainly respectable as her father was a Superior Court Judge. Paddy's father had bought them the house on Pacific Street as a wedding present and provided an income to support the maintenance and servant costs until Paddy inherited a substantial sum several years later. The William's marriage had produced two handsome sons to carry on the family tradition and both were away at Harvard and Yale working on the six-year graduation plan.

Upon hearing the doorbell ring, Pinky ran to let their guest in.

"Good evening Monsignor," he said with a slight bow.

"Pinky! Nice to see you are still here keeping the Williams in line." Al entered and handed Pinky his topcoat. He was wearing his collar and best suit, mostly so that the neighbors could see an esteemed cleric was visiting.

"The Master is fixing a drink in the library. I'm sure he would like you to join him," Pinky said as he put the coat away. Al knew the house well and headed toward the back library.

Al entered the sumptuous paneled room that contained shelves of rare books, two impressionist paintings on the wall, large bay windows that offered a view of the bay from the Golden Gate Bridge to Alcatraz and a hidden bar embedded behind several book shelves. "Paddy, how are you?"

"Al. You are a sight for sore eyes," Paddy said as he looked over his shoulder. "A little single malt, neat?"

Paddy handed him the drink and they shook hands. "Come sit. Becca will be down in a bit. So is this a visit or are you back for a while?"

"I am back for good. I have moved back into my old rooms at the cathedral and I have a new assignment." Al lifted his glass in a silent toast. "Surprised?"

"Yes. I thought you'd be in Rome forever, or perhaps made an archbishop somewhere. So what's your new assignment?" Paddy asked.

"Well my Rome adventure is a long story. I may tell it to you someday. But for now, the Archbishop has asked me to head up a new task force he is organizing, sort of a special project."

"Great. Sounds intriguing. I'd love to hear about it. I'm glad you're back though. I've missed out little talks. You are the only one I can be completely honest with about some parts of my life," Paddy said turning his head to look through the door and down the hallway. "Well, another time perhaps."

"Yes, of course, you bet. Perhaps we should schedule a nice long lunch, some place private," Al replied quietly.

"Ah Becca, look who the cat drug in," Paddy stood

up.

"Al, how lovely to see you again." Becca strode across the room and embraced Al with a kiss on each cheek. "Are we ready for dinner?"

"You look wonderful Becca, vibrant as always!"

Al followed his hosts into the solarium and held the chair out for Becca. As they sat, Pinky appeared with a soup course. Al said a blessing and they began to eat.

"Al has moved back permanently and has a new assignment, something very special it sounds like," Paddy began the conversation.

"Yes, and I'd be glad to tell you all about it, but first, how are you two? How are the kids?"

Becca proceeded to fill Al in on their recent vacation, how their boys were doing in school and some of her charity work. She was chatting away when Paddy interrupted her, "OK, enough about us, what are you up to Al?"

"OK, OK. But before I tell you, have you met the new archbishop? Tell me what you think of him." Al looked directly at Paddy.

"Oh, we've met him. He's OK, I guess. A little too conservative for my taste. As most Bishops do, he likes to talk rather than listen. He seems pretty taken with himself and his thoughts on matters. I don't have anything against him personally," Paddy replied.

Al looked at Becca. Now he would hear the unvarnished truth. She hesitated.

"Well. I think he's a complete horse's ass. Rude, chauvinistic, pompous and opinionated to a degree that shows him to be an idiot and a bore. And he is cruel. I don't think there is a Christian bone in his body," Becca said in a simple, quiet voice. "I'm sorry Al, but there it is. And you will hear the same from most of your old friends up here in the Heights. He's turned a lot of people off."

"I see. You know I respect your opinion. Can you give me some specifics?" Al asked, surprised at the vehemence of Becca's answer.

"Alright. Well, first. At the Catholic Charities fund raiser for unwed mothers, he was asked to speak a few words and regaled us with a talk about the dangers of condoms being available in the public schools and the evils of the morning after pill. My God, if the poor girls at St. Anne's Home had used birth control they wouldn't be there! Then, Shirley Bennett arrives, late due to her busy schedule of course, and HE gets up and leaves without so much as a "Hi, how are you?", a deliberate snub to Shirley in front of everyone. You can image how that played out among the audience. Shirley had the good manners not to say anything. It was unforgivably rude. She is such a devout Catholic and is always a top donor."

Al remembered that Shirley Bennett was the powerful congresswoman for San Francisco and the leader of California Democratic Party. She was known for her liberal positions on gay marriage and a women's right to choose.

"Finally, Spanky Fay hosted a welcome party for his 'highness' and invited everyone she knew to their home for an elaborate affair. Wonderfully catered by Gary Denko, valet parking, music by the Alexander String Quartet, it was an exquisite event. He gets up after a few drinks and says a couple of "Thank you's," then proceeds to lecture us on the need to defend marriage and the evils of the gay agenda. He goes on and on, standing right there next to Red and Spanky, and they with two out gay sons, who are lovely men. He didn't even notice all of us staring at the floor in embarrassment. Well, that was just cruel, to say nothing of very stupid. We were all mortified. He won't be dining with that crowd again I can assure you."

"I see." It was all Al could say.

"And Archbishop O'Brien was such a lovely man. I mean he was no raving liberal, but he didn't lecture us. He knew when to keep his mouth shut. He had proper manners. As you know all too well, many of us have been great financial supporters of the Archdiocese and its many good causes. This new man has effectively shut all that off. All the good work you did Al, in raising money for the Cathedral project, Catholic Charities, Hanna Boys Center, I could go on and on, and effectively using Archbishop O'Brien at the right moments, well it is sorely missed here now. If your new job is to front this new Archbishop's appeals you will have a rough time of it. I don't see how you can get him invited to any social event in the Heights. He is *persona non grata* among our friends. Who wants to be humiliated and insulted?"

"Thank you Becca for being so candid. I knew I could count on you to give me the straight scoop." Al picked up his glass and took a large gulp of wine. "In fact I have been brought back to San Francisco to help the Archbishop organize a new campaign, a program he envisions to make a major impact on serving the Latino community who he sees as the future of the Church. I can now begin to see why he needed my help so badly. I had no idea he had alienated so many of the Church's supporters. I know Red and Spanky too and their sons. I am chagrin to hear that story."

Becca frowned, took a sip of her wine and was about to speak when Paddy interrupted her. "Al, you know us and our crowd and you are respected here. You are always welcome and we will be open to what you might propose. But keep that man away. He's a nightmare. I've seen him several times now and he has no social sense. He can't read his audience and once you get him started on one of his pet peeves he goes on a tirade. He can't stop himself. I don't know how he got that job. I mean, who promoted him?"

"I have no idea. To be honest, I didn't even know he had been appointed until I got a letter from him in Rome," Al said, sounding deflated. "But I do appreciate your support and friendship."

They finished dinner with chitchat about various people they knew in common. Al begged off early to return back to the rectory. He was thoroughly depressed.

Back in his room, he took off his collar, changed his pants to jeans, mixed himself a double scotch and threw himself into the large easy chair in the corner of his room. After a large gulp of his drink, he stared around the room, a room that was all too familiar to him. "*What am I doing here?*" he asked himself. "*I'm right back where I started fifteen years ago, going nowhere and worse, stuck with the archbishop from hell.*" He looked down at his glass as it rested on his large stomach and felt disgust with himself. "*I'm fat and old and who would want me.*" He was thinking of a young boy of course.

He tried to cheer up by reminding himself what good friends Paddy and Becca were. There were many more like them who would welcome him into their homes, invite him to Stinson Beach or Napa for a weekend at their getaway house or even take him on vacation with them. But those relationships were always social and superficial. Al always had to play the priest role in one way or another and none of them knew his darkest secrets or vices, though if anyone, Paddy might suspect the focus of some of his desires. Once they had had a drunken conversation where Paddy had admitted he thought himself "really a bisexual." Al had admitted having slept with a man once in the seminary. In the morning afterward, they both complained of hangovers and that they couldn't remember going to bed the night before. Al remembered everything and assumed Paddy did too.

He fixed himself a second drink and tried to avoid the self-pity that was overtaking him. It was just three weeks since he had left Rome and he missed the privacy of living in his own apartment. Oddly, he was living with two other priests in the rectory, yet he felt more isolated living in the rectory that on his own. There was an unwritten rule that once a priest had retired for the night, no one would ever knock on the door of his three room suite, unless perhaps the place was burning down. In Rome, he could easily step out, go to a café for a drink and talk with the waiter or stop by one of his favorite clubs and eye the pretty boys at the bar or, if need be, slip into the backroom for a little grope or quick sex. It had been quite a while since he had hired a rent boy, mostly because he had made a vow to clean up his life under the influence and support of Brother Antonius. But now the healing work in the garden and the spiritual conversations with the Franciscan friar were becoming a distant memory. He just didn't have the willpower to fight his desires. He reasoned that watching a little porn and jacking off would be enough to quiet the urges. Then he could safely go to bed and sleep well.

The advances of the Internet had changed the nature of "watching a little porn." The wide variety of free porn and the ability to easily zero in on the specific focus of one's fantasies made it difficult to spend *just a little* time. Before he knew it, Al had found himself spending three or four hours in the middle of the night, finally dragging himself to bed in the wee hours of the morning. The Internet had also changed gay nightlife in San Francisco. There were a lot fewer gay bars and barely any clubs. "Hooking up" on line was the new method to find guys, a dance of seduction that Al didn't understand and had no skill at.

After an hour in front of the computer and finishing his third scotch, his desires grew more intense, not less. It wasn't yet eleven o'clock. He made the decision to search for a little company and was pleased to see that the Internet offered a wide variety of available escorts, each sporting their unique qualifications, physical vital statistics and availability to please. He didn't dare risk having anyone at the rectory but found many would host at their own place.

After two phone calls, he had set a date not far away and at a reasonable price of only $150. He grew excited at the prospects of enjoying the pleasures of Jake, a cute looking twink, young by his picture, who sounded very enticing on the phone. He decided not to have another drink before he left. He didn't want any performance issues. It had been well over a year since he had last been with anyone. As he put a sweater over his white shirt, he summoned up the splendid nights he had spent with Billy years ago, in this very room. To spend a few moments of bliss with a sweet young boy was all he wanted and needed.

By 12:30, he was back at the rectory. He headed directly to bed, exhausted and demoralized. He had forgotten that boys for rent wanted their money upfront and they watched the clock. It was a job for them. There was no passion. There was no connection. There was only the friction needed to reach a climax. Jake was young and sort of cute, but he and Al had not made the emotional connection that Al was looking for. Al had been unable to climax. Jake sported several tattoos of the devil and a rather bizarre one on his back that looked strikingly like a deformed serpent, which Al tried hard not to look at.

Back home, as he lay with his head on the pillow, he kept thinking about what Brother Antonius would think of him. Before dropping off to sleep, he made a vow to never go for another of those rent-boy rendezvous again. Even now, with the best of intentions, he wasn't sure that he could keep that vow. He worried he was spiraling down, as he had in Rome. He couldn't think of one helping hand that would lift him out of the cesspool he felt himself falling into. His depression finally brought sleep.

5

Billy tried to stay focused as he said the morning Mass, but all he could think about was that Al Pevehaus was coming to the rectory in the next hour to meet with him about the Archbishop's new fund drive. He was anxious because he had so many mixed feelings. He looked forward to seeing his old love obsession, yet he knew that Al was not trustworthy, and he would have to be on his guard. Billy reminded himself that he was a grown man now, not the boy that Al had seduced in high school. He wanted to be treated as an equal, yet secretly he always liked it when Al took charge. It had been two years since their last encounter at the Vatican. They had parted friends and had reconciled over the trauma of their early years together in San Francisco, but still Billy was unsure how they would deal with each other on this new project.

Billy was having a cup of coffee with Father Red at the

kitchen table when the doorbell rang. Billy looked at Red with raised eyebrows.

"That's probably him."

"Yeah, well, I'll let you two get your work done," Red said, as he got up. Before he could leave, Al appeared at the door of the kitchen dressed in his most formal clerical suit.

"Hello Al, how are you?" Red reached out his hand.

"My God, Red Reilly! How are you? It's been years since we've seen each other. You don't look a day older, how do you do it?" Al said, vigorously shaking Red's hand.

"Clean living I suppose," Red replied. "It looks as though that Roman pasta agreed with you though. How's it feel to be back in San Francisco?"

"Great. Yes, I'm on a new diet. Time to lose a few pounds. I didn't know you were stationed here. You must be the pastor," Al said with a big smile to hide the hurt he felt at Red's noticing his weight gain.

"That's what they tell me. But here is the star of the parish. I think you two know each other." Red gestured toward Billy and made his way toward to the door. "I'll let you two get to it. Good to see you, Al. Welcome back."

"Hello Billy, how's life in the Mission going?" Al said, sounding upbeat.

"Great, I love it. Would you like a cup of coffee?" Billy shook Al's hand and noticed it was a bit sweaty, not unlike his own. "I guess he's nervous too," Billy thought to himself. Somehow that made him relax.

"Sure. Where shall we meet?"

"How about right here?"

"Well, maybe some place a little more private."

"Okay. I don't really have an office. I suppose we could meet in my room." Billy didn't like that idea, but he really had no choice if Al wanted total privacy. A thought passed through his head that Al deliberately wanted to get Billy into his bedroom.

They both grabbed their coffees and headed upstairs. Billy's room was a typical two room suite, one a bedroom and the other a sort of parlor with a couch, a chair and an old TV that he never watched.

Al sat on the couch, Billy in the chair.

"So isn't it ironic that we should be working together on this project? How did you get roped into it?" Al asked.

"I opened my big mouth, that's how. The Archbishop was here for a visit and over lunch asked me several questions about the needs of the Latino community in the Mission and the next thing I knew I was on this special project. He wants me to do some kind of a survey to find out what people really want from the Church," Billy said, trying to sound positive even though he hated the whole idea.

"Yes, and he wants me to take that information and raise a bunch of money from the well-heeled of Pacific Heights."

Billy stared at Al with a curious look, "Well-heeled?"

"Yes, the super rich. It's a slang term," Al answered back. "It's not going to be easy. The Archbishop has succeeded in alienating a lot them in the short time he has been here."

"Oh."

"Have you figured out yet how you are going to do this survey? Have you ever done one?" Al asked.

"No. And I have no idea where to even start. Do you?"

"Not really, I haven't done one myself but I know some-one, a professional who can help us. It may cost some money but it would be well-documented and probably pretty accu-rate. If it's really well done, it would help in the bigger fund raising work." There was a pause in the conversation as they looked at each other.

"You seem good Billy. You've grown into a fine looking man. Are you happy here? And how is your mother?" Al asked in rapid fire.

"Yes, I am. Thanks for asking. My mother is doing quite well. She has her little community of old ladies down on 24th Street and loves that I'm back near her." Billy was touched that Al remembered to ask about his mother. He relaxed and softened towards the man. "How are you doing? Is it strange to be back?"

"Oh, I'm okay. Not great. I'm back in my own rooms at the Cathedral, which is like I have come full circle. I was tired of Rome and pretty restless, so I was happy to get a call to come back to San Francisco. But this new Archbishop is not quite what I had expected. He's sort of a jerk and very conservative. It's not an act that plays well in San Francisco. From what I've heard from some of my friends, he's pretty insensitive to people. Got a thing about gay folks too." Al looked close at Billy to gage his response.

"Yes, I know what you mean. He really brow beat me into taking this assignment. I think he likes me though, which may be more of a curse than a benefit," Billy replied.

"Well, it could be worse. But I don't have to tell you to be careful. You know how quickly a prelate's favorite can change overnight if you don't do what he wants."

"Yes, I know," he said, thinking of his experiences with Al as a teenager.

The Monsignor followed his train of thought and looked away uncomfortably. "Okay, well, here is my idea. I'll contact my friend who knows about surveys and come back to you with some proposals. Once we get an idea about the cost,

I'll set about a way to get the money. You may need to help with that. I'll let you know. I should be back to you in about a week. Once we get the survey done, we can then concentrate on turning the findings into specific programs that would then become the basis of the bigger fundraising task. My thought is that we should be ready for that part within about three months," Al stated in his most professional manner.

"You certainly have a better idea about this than I do. I was completely lost as to what to do next and where it was all going to go. I think I might learn a thing or two from you on this job." Billy said, "Thanks," with a sigh of relief.

"I've done this kind of thing a hundred times. It's old hat to me. I'm glad we are working together Billy. I never dreamed we would see each other again after that disaster in Rome. It's a real surprise." Al stood, took a last sip of his coffee, set the cup down and turned to leave.

He turned back to Billy. "By the way, you haven't heard from your uncle Jorge have you?"

"No, I haven't. And I don't expect to. I'm sure he is not happy with either of us," Billy replied with a frown. "I've cut off all communication with the family. They were just using me anyway."

"Good. I never want to see or hear from him again either. Hopefully we are safe here."

"Thanks Al." Billy gave him a hug, which surprised Al. He returned the gesture warmly.

"Talk with you soon."

Billy took the coffee cups back to the kitchen after seeing Al to the front door. Red was pouring himself another cup.

"So, how did it go?" he asked.

"Good. Al seems to know what he is doing in all this and he is going to get a professional to help me do this survey. I feel better about it," Billy replied.

"He looks terrible. I haven't seen him in a number of years. He's gained a lot of weight, and the booze is starting to show in his face, all puffy and blotched. He's pretty shaky too. I was shocked at how bad he looks," Red said with a concerned look on his face.

"I think he has a lot of vices," Billy said looking away. "I guess they take their toll."

"Yes they do," Red said as he walked out of the kitchen.

Billy thought about what Red had said. He liked to remember Al as he was when they first met, when Billy was in high school: handsome, fit, confident, so assured and articulate with people, yet warm and comforting. Billy had wanted everything that Al was. He loved the attention, the nurturing and affection that he had felt from him. In many ways, the person Billy had become was the embodiment of those early desires. He had to admit now though that Al had seriously deteriorated, at least in his looks. He had discovered in Rome some of Al's peculiar vices, the drugs, the boys and the excessive drinking. He knew why Al appeared to be falling apart. If he didn't change his ways, then the decline was only going to get worse and Billy was concerned, both for Al and how it might affect him.

6

Al's new Mercedes S550 black sedan looked quite out of place as it pulled up to the front of the rectory at Mission Dolores. He phoned Billy to let him know he was outside to pick him up. Soon the car door opened and Billy got in.

"I see you still like flashy cars. Is it new?" Billy asked with a slightly cynical tone.

"Just picked it up yesterday. Nice huh?"

"Yeah, sure. So where are we going?"

"To a friend's house for dinner. I think they might fund the study. Did you get the proposal by email? I brought it with me," Al replied.

"Yes, I read it. Steve seemed to get the concept and presented a very professional approach to getting the survey done in the next ninety days. I was amazed because we really only had that one phone call."

Al had contacted Steve Sayer of Survey Source Associates, who after a one-hour conference call had put together a proposal to develop, conduct and package a survey of 500 people in the Mission District.

"He's very good. I used him on the Cathedral project and at Catholic Charities, so I really trust his work. I called him later and got him to lower his price down to $35,000, half of what he wanted to charge," Al said, boasting a little.

"So who are these friends and why do I need to be there?" Billy asked.

"They are old friends of mine. They are quite wealthy and live in Pacific Heights. We are having dinner at their house. I want them to meet you. I think the fact that you are heading up the survey and are our entrée into the Latin community is very important to give this whole idea some credibility. Plus, they had a terrible experience with the Archbishop. You are just the antidote to the bad taste they still have in their mouth about him. You'll like them. They are nice people and easy to talk to," Al said as he speeded up a hilly street toward Pacific Street.

"If they are old friends of yours, why are we dressed up like we are meeting the Pope?" Billy asked with a bit of aggression in his voice.

"Well, it's only proper we dress as priests. Besides, the neighbors are all nosey, and it's good that we are known to be visiting. It's all part of the game. Trust me, I know what I'm doing. You'll learn," Al replied, looking aside at Billy with a knowing grin.

Pinky the houseboy answered the door and bowed slightly to Al. "Good evening, Monsignor."

"Hello Pinky. This is my colleague Father Hernandez. Are we early?"

"Nice to meet you, Father. No, you aren't early. The madam just asked me if you had arrived. May I take your coat?"

"Are we eating inside or in the garden?" Al asked.

"In the garden tonight," Pinky answered.

"Well, we'll keep our coats thank you."

Al proceeded into the house toward the library. "Are they in the library?"

"Yes."

Billy marveled at the immense size of the entry hallway, glancing to his right at the parlor, which was filled with antiques. He stayed close to Al who was proceeding at full pace. As they entered the paneled library, Al reached back and pushed Billy forward.

"Paddy, I want you to meet Father Billy Hernandez. Billy, this is John Williams."

"A pleasure to meet you Father," John said, giving Billy a firm handshake and a deep look into his eyes. "Al and I go way back, and you are one of few priests he has ever introduced us to."

"Well, Billy and I go back a ways too. I knew him when he was just a high school student here at Cathedral High. We lost touch, but then got reacquainted in Rome a couple of years ago," Al said, beaming with a bit of pride.

"Really? You studied in Rome?" John asked with a very warm and broad smile.

"Yes. I went to the Mexican college at the Vatican," Billy answered.

"Billy was actually ordained by our new Holy Father, just after he was elected Pope," Al interjected.

"My, what an honor. Were you ordained in St. Peter's?"

"Yes. My mother, who lives here in San Francisco, was overjoyed, and a bit overwhelmed too."

"I can only imagine," John replied, not taking his eyes off Billy.

Pinky cleared his throat ever so slightly.

"Gentlemen, pardon my rudeness. Please give Pinky your drink requests and sit down. Becca will be down in a few minutes," John said, taking his cue from Pinky.

"I'll have whatever Paddy is having, I trust his good taste," Al answered. He sat himself down on the couch.

"A diet coke for me," Billy said looking a little confused at Al.

"Paddy is John's nick name. And he always drinks the very best single malt scotch," Al said.

John gestured to Billy to sit in the chair slightly opposite his.

"So tell me Father, why did you study at the Mexican college? Are you Mexican? I don't hear even the slightest accent in your English," John said sitting across from Billy, leaning forward and seeming to take him in as the most important person in the room.

"Yes. I was born in Mexico and came to San Francisco when I was twelve. I went back after high school. I studied at the Catholic University in Monterrey, Mexico and then went to the seminary in Rome. I asked to come to San Francisco after ordination and have been back about a year already," Billy answered, enjoying the attention John was giving him.

"Fascinating. We are so blessed to have you here in San Francisco. Where are you assigned?"

"Mission Dolores."

There was a motion at the door of the library and John stood up. "Becca, please meet Father Billy Hernandez. He works with Al."

"Pleased to meet you, Father. Hello, Al darling, how are you?" Becca said, first shaking hands with Billy and then giving Al a kiss on the cheek. "My, but you are a handsome young priest. Where, oh where, did you meet this fine young fellow Al?" Becca asked teasingly. Pinky arrived with their drinks.

"Believe it or not, I have known Billy since high school and we also knew each other in Rome. Now he is working here in the Mission. But I'll have more to tell you about that during dinner. How is everything in your world?" Al said, trying to take a bit of the focus off Billy.

"Oh, everything is good here. The boys are still away and I've been busy preparing for the symphony gala. My God, that is such work! I think John is a bit bored though, you should find something for him to do." Becca laughed lightly.

"Tell us about your work in the Mission Father," John asked earnestly. He looked admiringly at Billy.

"Oh, it's just regular parish work, mass, baptisms, weddings and funerals, but I have also been working to support the New Hope Recovery House. Have you heard of it?" Billy asked John.

"No, I haven't. Tell me about it."

"It was started by a very special nun, Sister Jane Matthews, who is a Social Services sister. It offers help to those most in need of support. Battered women, men and women with addictions issues, kids turned out of their families for various reasons, families trying to stay off the streets. She does marvelous work."

"I see. That all sounds very interesting. Perhaps we could support her financially, I'm sure there is a need there." John leaned closer to Billy.

"You should come down for a visit. I would be glad to go with you, introduce you to her and show you around," Billy said, leaning toward John.

"Hey, I thought I was the money grubbing priest around here," Al interjected, trying to make a joke. "You are supposed to be learning from me."

"Well, he has certainly peaked John's interest," Becca said to Al. "John, honey, you should go for a visit. You need a new interest. Perhaps you can help in other ways too, I mean, besides just writing a check."

Pinky silently appeared. "Dinner is served."

They adjourned to the large deck behind the house that melded into a lush garden of flowers, shrubs and trees. A table was set at the far end of the deck, which afforded a beautiful vista of the San Francisco Bay from the Golden Gate Bridge to Alcatraz Island. Although outside, the table was set as if for a formal dining experience, with fine silver, candles and a beautiful floral arrangement in the center. Once seated, John and Billy continued speaking about the center while Becca and Al caught up on gossip of the Pac Heights crowd. The first course was a fresh crab cake salad with ripe Sonoma peaches. John had Pinky bring out a rare French Chablis for Billy to taste. He boasted that it was one of only fifty bottles produced and would be perfect with the salad. As the main course of chateaubriand served with a chanterelle risotto and an asparagus tart was presented, Billy looked across the table at Al and rolled his eyes with a big grin that said he was enjoying the whole rich dinner experience.

"Bringing back some memories Billy?" Al asked.

"Yes, it does."

"Billy was secretary to an important cardinal in Rome for a short time. Cardinal Lucelli was a friend of mine as well.

He was known to have one of the best private chefs in all of Italy, so we both have experience with some very special meals. But this one is right up there with the best of those, don't you think?"

"Yes, by all means. This setting is far beyond anything in Rome," Billy said, with a slight toast of his glass. "As are our hosts."

"Why, thank you." Becca returned the toast, obviously taken with Billy's successful attempt at charm. John simply smiled a broad grin as he watched Billy.

"Well, now that we are all feeling good, and I must say this dinner is exquisite, I do have a bit of an agenda," Al said as he continued to eat. "I spoke with you both several weeks ago about a new project I was working on. Billy and I would like to present the outline of it to you for any helpful comments you might have."

"Fine Al, as long as you don't mention the name of that man at the Cathedral," Becca warned.

"No, this is all about Billy and me. We have been tasked with doing a survey of the needs of the Latino community in San Francisco to determine what the focus of the Church should be, to better serve that growing and important segment of the city. We hope the survey will give us concrete data to better build the right services and institutions to more fully integrate that community into the city and the life of the Church. We have a well-known professional group that will design the survey and compile the data afterwards," Al stated.

"I'm sure I know what your role is Al, but tell me Father Hernandez, what will be your role in this project?" John asked.

"I...," Billy started to answer but was interrupted by Al.

"Father Hernandez is our entrée into the Latino community. He will present the survey to various groups in the community and will sell them on participating and giving us honest answers to the questions. He has built an excellent reputation in a short amount of time and is a trusted priest, especially among those that may not be here legally."

"I see. That sounds very smart," John said.

"Yes, that will be my role," Billy added.

"And so, I was hoping to interest you two in the role of funding the fees to get the survey created and compiled," Al added quickly with a smile, looking at both John and Becca.

"How much?" Becca asked.

"$35,000."

"Of course, we would be happy to," John blurted out immediately. Becca raised her eyebrows and looked at John. He had not even looked her way to see what she thought.

"Well, I guess that's settled," Becca spoke. "Now we can enjoy dessert."

"Thank you both so much, I knew I could count on you. I think this will be a very important donation. It may change the city and even the church in countless ways that will make you proud and grateful to have played a critical part in it. We are both very grateful," Al said reaching out to touch Becca's arm.

"Then I guess we will be seeing more of you Father Hernandez," John said smiling.

"Please, call me Billy, we are working together as a team, I don't think we need to be quite so formal," Billy replied.

"So why do you call yourself Billy? I assume that is not your given name," John asked.

"Well, when I came here, I wanted to fit into American society. My real name is Guillermo, which is Spanish for William, and so I picked the nickname of Billy. It's my American name and made it a lot easier in high school. I like it, so I've kept it," Billy explained.

"Well, then you can call me Paddy, and, of course, Becca. I think we are off to a great new friendship," John said reaching out to Billy's shoulder.

As Billy and Al drove off, they waved to John and Becca who were standing on the front porch.

"Well, I guess that went pretty well," Billy said.

"Yes, it was all perfect. You presented yourself quite well, I must say. That Roman training certainly showed through," Al replied.

"They are such wonderful people, very gracious and certainly generous."

"John was very much taken with you. He couldn't take his eyes off you. I think you have a new friend," Al said, glancing sideways at Billy.

"He is so handsome, so warm and kind. We are getting together next week to visit New Hope and meet Sister Jane."

"I don't think I have ever seen John so responsive to someone new. He is usually standoffish, but not with you. If I didn't know better I would say he was smitten."

"Yes, well Becca is nice too," Billy said trying to deflect the implications of Al's comment.

"She is. But John's not a hugger and he gave you a rather long hug goodbye. I suppose I can't blame him," Al replied shrugging his shoulders. They rode the rest of the way back to Mission Dolores in silence.

7

Two weeks later, Billy received a phone call from Al that surprised him.

"Hey. I have a tough assignment for you," Al said in a jovial manner.

"Oh no, now what?" Billy answered.

"How'd you like to spend a week in Hawai'i, all expenses paid, furthering our little survey project?"

"Al, what are you talking about? What tricks have you been up to?" Billy answered trying to sound like he was joking, but actually he was worried.

"Well, Paddy and Becca asked me to join them on a family trip to Kauai next month, but I can't go. The Archbishop has assigned me to do an audit of Mercy Hospital and it's scheduled to take place the week they are going. They were very insistent that I ask you to take my place instead. Can you get away for a week? It's important that we keep these folk involved in the project and you need to do your part in that."

"Are you sure? They want me?"

"Becca was adamant."

"Really? I'll have to ask Red but I've been here almost a year and a half and I haven't taken any vacation. I've never been to Hawai'i. What's it like?" Billy asked trying not to show his growing enthusiasm.

"It's paradise. They have rented a house right on the beach on the north shore. The water is deliciously warm, the beaches long and mostly empty, and it's beautiful. I've been several times and love it. I'm jealous that you are going and I'm not," Al replied.

"Who else is going?"

"Just you, Becca, John and the two boys, but they are gone everyday surfing on Poipu beach on the south side of the island. You probably won't see much of them."

"Okay, I'll check. But I'm excited. Do I have to do anything to earn my keep?"

"Yeah, say grace before dinner."

The long flight to Kauai went by quite quickly as they all flew first class, something that Billy had never experienced. The four course meal and a bit too much of the crisp white wine induced Billy to nap and before he realized it they were landing. They walked down to the Hertz rental car counter and signed for two large SUVs when suddenly Pinky appeared with their luggage on a large cart that was topped with two surfboards. Billy had not even noticed him on the plane; obviously he did not fly first class with the rest of the family. He had met the two William's boys, John Jr. who was called Scooter and Paul, whose nick-name was Rusty at the gate before leaving San Francisco, but they were absorbed in the games on their iPads and took little notice of him during the flight. The boys and Pinky loaded the boards and suitcases into one SUV and took off down the road.

After an hours drive through breathtaking scenery, they arrived at Anini Beach and pulled into a long circular driveway. There stood a large modern glass structure with a veranda porch that surrounded the entire front of the house. Stepping inside, Billy was amazed at the architecture. Every room featured floor to ceiling windows, with the front of the house presenting verdant gardens full of exotic flowers, flowing ferns and multiple palm trees, all of which stunned Billy by their tropical lushness. The back of the house had a full view of the beach and sea. A gentle cooling breeze, blowing in from the ocean, cooled the warm, humid air. The effect was of complete relaxation and a much slower pace of life. Having never been in any climate like the tropics, Billy tried to take it all in. He couldn't stop exclaiming how beautiful it was. He was so grateful for the invitation.

"Okay, you've thanked us enough. Now, Becca don't you think we need to get this young man properly outfitted?" John said clasping Billy's shoulder, "He's dressed as if the freezing San Francisco fog will roll in any minute, which will never happen here."

"Yes, of course. Why don't you take Billy into Hanalei and see what they have. I want to help Pinky unpack and get cracking on my novel," Becca replied, sauntering off toward her bedroom.

Billy hadn't known what to pack. He wore a pair of jeans on the plane and a white long sleeve shirt. His suitcase held three pairs of black pants, a clerical shirt and a couple of T-shirts. Billy never really had a need for casual clothes before; he didn't even own a swimsuit.

"I do need to buy a swim suit," he said to John.

"Don't worry, we'll fix you up."

They drove into Hanalei, a small old Hawaiian village nestled along the beach. John found a high-end clothing store behind an upscale restaurant.

"Please now, Billy, you are our guest, and it would be my pleasure to buy you some vacation clothes. I hope you won't be offended. I know you don't make much money as a priest, so let's just make this fun and easy," John said, again touching Billy's shoulder affectionately.

"Okay, I want to be comfortable and I want you to be too."

"Good. First, let's look at shorts, then shirts, swimsuits, uh, sandals of course, and finally a hat. I've got it all figured out."

Three large bags and two thousand dollars later, Billy felt slightly overwhelmed by the freedom with which John spent money. Price never seemed to matter. Even when he was Al's favorite in high school and Al always paid for everything, there wasn't the sense that money was in inexhaustible supply. Billy found himself almost dizzy by this new experience of wealth.

They returned to the house, got into their swimsuits and headed to the beach. The water was a comfortable 80 degrees and the waves only slight. They swam out quite a way, yet Billy was surprised that he could still feel the sandy bottom and stand even hundreds of feet from the shore.

"This is *fabuloso!*" Billy shouted to John. They splashed a little water onto each other and laughed. They floated on their backs and bumped heads.

"Hey, watch it!" John said and shoved Billy underwater by his shoulders. Billy came up quickly and reached over to push John down under, but he was standing and didn't move.

"No fair!" Billy said laughingly and then proceeded to wrestle him. Eventually Billy got John off balance and he went under.

"OK, OK, now we are even," John said, coming up, gulping for air. "You are too strong for me."

They swam a little longer and then headed for shore. After drying off, they sat under a small grove of palm trees at the edge of the beach. Billy told John how he finally learned to swim at the university, a requirement for graduation. John asked more about his university days and Billy told him of his aunt and Sister Immaculata, a nun who became a close friend. Eventually, Billy explained how he had been arrested by the Immigration Service in San Francisco just as he finished high school and was deported back to Mexico. He spoke of his rescue by a young nun and his aunt. It was the nun's order that sponsored a full scholarship to enter the university.

John sat listening intently, unable to take his eyes off Billy for even a second. He was enraptured by Billy's story and the courage he showed to build his life. "You are an amazing man," he finally said.

"Thank you. Just lucky and blessed. God has been so very good to me," Billy replied, trying not to blush. He was enjoying the attention by an established and confident older man, especially the warm eye contact and gentle smile John had shown throughout the day. "Tell me of your life."

"Well, mine is a very different story. I grew up in privilege. My family is an old and established one in San Francisco with great wealth and status. We have been the models of society for generations, even though we were Catholic. Everything has been handed to me on a silver platter. As long as I did what I was told of course," John said looking deeply at Billy.

He turned away and stared out at the ocean. "To be very honest, it has been a lonely life in ways that I am just beginning to discover."

"Really, how so?" Billy asked quietly.

"Like many wealthy families throughout history, I was actually raised by my nanny, who I called Pippa. She was a sweet and loving lady in many ways, but very formal too. It was her job to make sure that I grew up to be the model of what my parents wanted for me. I would never be an embarrassment to them. I learned to conform at a young age to be what my elders expected of me and that I fulfilled the demands of the family heritage. I rarely saw my parents, oh on special occasions and holidays of course, but they were so social that there was always a crowd of people around. Being the only child, everything was pinned on me to fulfill their expectations. My father and I probably only had five conversations alone and those were so he could tell me what to do. Mother was the consummate socialite, involved in every charity and always preferred the company of women. So here I am at fifty-five, still fulfilling their expectations, and I find that I don't really know who I am. I have all the money in the world, but I don't know what I really want to do with my life. I have fulfilled the role of husband, father and head of the family, but inside I feel very alone, and I'm wondering, when do I get to live?" John turned to Billy who was looking at him with care and attention. He was hit with a tremendous feeling of being loved, that someone was really listening to him and not judging in any way. John was befuddled and didn't know what to do with the feeling and the intense connection he was experiencing with Billy at that moment. "Listen to me, going on. I'm telling you way more than you asked. Sorry." He broke the connection and kicked some sand away.

"No. Please don't stop. I understand what you are saying. I know I am a lot younger, but I understand the loneliness of living up to other's expectations. But I think I hear you saying something that is deeper, a sort of spiritual crisis. You feel the deep need to come out of the shadows and show the real you, to live more authentically than you ever have." Billy spoke in a soothing voice and placed his hand on top of John's.

John kept very still and let the hand stay on his. He leaned closer to Billy and smiled faintly, with a small quiver in his lips, and looked longingly into his eyes. "Thank you. That is so sweet of you to say. Perhaps I am. I know that lately I'm feeling like I just want to jump out of my skin. I have fantasies of running away and taking on a new identity, starting life over. But I can't. They are just day dreams." Slightly embarrassed, he looked away down the beach. "I have never spoken like this with anyone before but you are such a good listener, I find it easy to tell you. I'm afraid my friends, even the dear Monsignor, would find it a shock to hear such things coming out of my mouth."

"There you two are!" shouted Becca from behind the trees as Billy quickly lifted his hand. "It's getting to cocktail hour and I need a drink. Dinner will be in about an hour. Pinky has thoughtfully hired a local chef to cook for us and she has been slaving away in the kitchen creating a real welcome feast. Did you go for a swim?"

"Yes Becca, it was marvelous," John said and quickly stood up. "Come on Billy, we'll shower and show off some of your new duds."

They walked back to the house, John with his arm around Becca's shoulders.

8

Billy quickly learned that each of the Williams had a set idea of what their vacation should be. Scooter and Rusty slept until noon, then ate and went off to surf until dinner. Becca lounged all day around the house or on the deck, reading pulp romance novels. John was the activist, always intent to do something outdoors or on the water. It became Billy's role to join John and keep him company. Every day was a different endeavor and a new experience for Billy. Kayaking, sailing, snorkeling, hiking, biking and then swimming. Not that he minded, but even though he was twenty-seven, Billy had a tough time keeping up with John, who was a very fit fifty-five.

John was unfailingly patient with Billy as he learned each new skill. He taught him how to paddle the kayak, efficiently to go on long voyages up the coast, in the open ocean without getting overly tired and how to recover if thrown over.

The first day out, they viewed the waterfalls several miles up the Napali coast. They went into the caves where the giant sea turtles laid their eggs and surfed the waves on the afternoon tides. On the second day, he taught him the rudiments of sailing on a Hobie Cat catamaran and by the afternoon, Billy was accomplished enough to sail all the way back to Hanalei from Lighthouse Point. Snorkeling was the easiest to learn. The reefs just off Anini Beach provided ample opportunity to view hundreds of different species of fish, an experience that so entranced Billy, John had to order him to get out of the water after five long hours of exploring the entire reef. The salt water had begun to cause a rash on Billy's skin. They rented mountain bikes and traveled the back roads of the Waimea Canyon Park. The next day, they hiked for seven hours along the coastal trail up to the midpoint of the Napali Coast Lookout.

The days flew by. Each night, as he lay in bed exhausted and parched by the sun and fresh air, Billy said a prayer of gratitude for the day and for John. Each day was more amazing that the previous one. He had never had so many intense, new experiences in so short a time. He conceded to himself that the best part of every day was basking in the attention of an older man, relishing the care and tutoring of an accomplished and confident person who seemed to find delight in every moment he spent with Billy. He reflected that it was like a few early memories he had of his father, tragically cut short by his murder when Billy was ten.

Billy and John talked a good deal during the day, about many things, but there was never the level of intimacy that they shared the first day on the beach. They spoke more of their family histories, John's boredom as an attorney, the Roman seminary experience and Billy's work with Father Filiberto at the garbage dump in Rome, John and Becca's romance at university and other personal parts of their life stories. Billy was careful not to mention his affair with Al in high school or the drug cartel connection of his uncle, both parts of his life that he was ashamed of. Yet with these secrets kept, the hours spent together having fun and talking for hours on end, created a strong bond between them that grew in its intensity every day.

On the morning of his last full day in Hawai'i, Billy awoke to another intense sexual dream in which he was wild-ly fucking a muscular man who, between moans, kept saying "Thank you, oh thank you." Billy could not see his face, but he was familiar. He shook himself awake before he climaxed and found himself so aroused he immediately grabbed his erection and with two short strokes came over his chest and stomach. As he lay panting on his bed, he wondered who the man was. Why couldn't he see the face? He thought about the body. He could clearly visualize the strong arms and the hands holding his face and the slightly-hairy chest pressed against his and the knobby knees that stuck out as strong legs were wrapped around him. The body was familiar. He lay quiet for a few minutes, reliving the dream and then it struck him. It was John's body. He didn't know what to do with that thought. He wanted to be ashamed, but he wasn't. In the dream, he was clearly enjoying himself, as was John.

He pushed the thought of sex with John out of his head and willed himself to stop thinking of it. But he kept reflect-ing on John and his relationship. Billy had experienced a close connection with only two other men, Al and Filiberto, both priests. They were of course not married and while there was never a sexual relationship with Filiberto, both were sacred to him in some idealized way, a measure that Billy thought led him to something holy and to goodness. But John was just an ordinary family man, albeit a wealthy and accomplished one, not one with a divine mission or a sacred connection to the church. This bond with a regular man was something new and it made him feel different. Living with John every day in the exotic otherworld of Hawai'i, Billy could be himself in a new way. He did not have to play the role of priest. He hadn't even said grace before dinner as Al had suggested. Their conversations, about their lives, sometimes included profanity and never broached the subject of religion or the church. Here, he did not have to fulfill the obligations or expectations of being holy, of belonging to a separate and sacred class of man. Instead, he could be an ordinary person, himself. There was a freedom in it that he had never felt before. Added to this new feeling was a confusing consternation that John was obviously a straight man who might be offended or scandalized if he knew of Billy's dream and erotic attraction. Billy could never confess that he was gay.

He got out of bed and headed to the shower. It was nearly 9 a.m. John and Becca would already be finishing their breakfast and John would certainly have a plan for the day.

Pinky placed a large cheese omelet and fresh fruit in front of him.

"Thank you Pinky," Billy looked up and smiled. There was no one else at the table.

"You are welcome Father," came the reply with a slight smile. "The Master asks that you meet him across the way on the beach when you are finished."

Over the week, Billy had found that Pinky made him feel increasingly uneasy. It wasn't just that he was not used to being waited on, but that at the house Pinky was invisible yet omnipresent. He seemed to know everything that was going on in the family and at the house. He knew every family member so well that he anticipated their every need, even before they would think it. He would appear just when needed then disappear. Billy had the notion that Pinky could even read their minds and know their every feeling. Nothing could ever be hidden from the houseboy. Billy hardly saw him, except at meals. He was everywhere, but he never stood out. He wondered what Pinky thought of him. What might Pinky be thinking of the close relationship that had developed between him and John?

Billy found John laying on the beach sunning himself and was aroused by seeing the body that had been so real in his dream just an hour before.

"Hi, what's up for today?"

"Good morning, Billy. I thought that since you loved snorkeling so much we might explore another beach that has a nice reef. It's very secluded so we need to drive, then hike for quite a bit to get there. It's called Neptune Beach," John replied jumping up.

"Great, let's do it."

After parking the car on a small dirt road, they hiked down a thin trail through heavy brush. After twenty minutes, Billy saw a small, isolated cove emerging. There appeared to be no access except the path they were on. The water had a green hue that washed upon a glistening white sand beach, surrounded by a thick forest of trees and dense undergrowth. In the middle of the horseshoe shape of the cove, he could see the outline of a reef.

"Oh my God, this is paradise!" exclaimed Billy.

"I thought you'd like it. It's worth the trouble to get here. I doubt we'll see another soul all day."

They laid down their backpacks in the shade of a loulu

palm and set out a towel.

"I'm sweating bullets. If you don't mind, I'm going to jump in and cool off." John instantly stripped off his shoes, pants and shirt. "I don't have time to find my swimsuit."

Billy watched him run toward the water, his white butt cheeks flashing against his tanned back and legs. He was entranced but hesitant. He threw away caution and joined in. As he stripped down, he felt a thrill in the pit of his stomach, which caused him to stumble as he frantically tried to get his shoes off, falling onto the sand. Finally nude, he ran to the water as fast as he could. He hoped the excitement at being naked with John wouldn't make him too hard.

John swam out toward the middle of the lagoon, then flipped over on his back and began floating. Billy swam towards him.

"I've never swam naked in the ocean before," he said as he approached John.

John sank underwater and surfaced, face to face with Billy. He asked, "Doesn't it feel great?"

"It does. Like everything else this week."

John reached out his hand and put it on Billy's head. "You've made this the best vacation I have ever had. You are so much fun to be with, I feel like I'm back in my twenties," John said smiling and laughing. He spit a mouthful of water at Billy.

"Hey, watch it!" Billy said, taking a gulp of water and spitting it back in John's face.

"Oh, you little brat!" John reached over and dunked him under. Billy came up and reached for John and they immediately started to wrestle, but the water was deep and they both sank under the turquoise surface.

"OK, OK, I give!" John shouted, "You're too strong."

John started to swim toward the beach. Billy followed, but swam slower because now he knew he had an erection.

Billy stayed in the water a little longer while John got out and walked toward their backpacks. He reached into his bag and brought out his swimsuit and put it on. Finally when Billy thought it safe, he got out of the water and did the same. He noticed John watching him while pretending not to.

"Let's eat something, then after a rest, go find some fish. I'm hungry."

"OK," Billy replied.

After they had eaten the sandwiches Pinky had packed, they lay on their towels next to each other and soaked up the sun. After resting for a half hour, John jumped up. "Come on, let's not waste the day."

They spent nearly three hours exploring the reef, signaling to each other when a new species of fish was spotted, making hand gestures to try to communicate their thoughts. It was nearing late afternoon when they dragged themselves out of the water and back to the towels.

"That was just amazing! I couldn't believe the bright red color of that small pointy nose fish. We saw so many different kinds together. But I'm exhausted," John said as he sat down.

"Me too. Time for a nap." They lay down again and dozed off.

John shook Billy slightly to waken him. "Look," he said pointing out to the ocean slightly to the right of them. Far out to sea was a large billowing cloud formation and a brilliant reddish orange sun falling behind it that sent rays of light shooting up into the sky. The few, small clouds floating closer to them took on a pinkish tinge. The water lost its greenish hue and was now deep blue. They stared silently at the setting sun, hunched on their elbows.

Billy was looking at him. "John, this is the most beautiful day of my life. I love you." He spoke, almost without realizing what he had said.

John looked down into Billy's eyes with the most grateful smile and slowly leaning down, kissed him softly on the lips. "I love you, too."

They separated, looking at each other, lovingly. Billy reached up, grabbed John's head by the hair and gave him a deep, long and passionate kiss. John did not pull back or hesitate. He eagerly kissed him back. Within seconds they were intertwined, with John on top, kissing each other deeply and frantically. Billy rolled John over and lay on top. He kissed John's chest and shoulders, then his neck and ears. John moaned and held Billy tight.

"Oh my God, you feel so good," John whispered. "I've wanted to kiss you all week, but was so afraid you would be shocked and offended."

"I've been dreaming of you doing just that," Billy murmured into John's ear.

They kissed intently again though more slowly and with care. Afterward, Billy laid his head on John's chest while John ran his fingers through Billy's hair. They lay still for a minute, then John rolled Billy onto his back and reached down to push his swimsuit off.

"Are you sure?" Billy asked.

"Oh, I'm sure," John answered. He took off his own suit.

John crawled back on top of Billy, kissing him with new passion. He then began to kiss Billy's chest, licking his right nipple, caressing the other with his fingers, and winding his tongue down the center of his tight abs, moving deliberately down to the prize. He took him fully into his mouth and Billy moaned with pleasure. John too was completely absorbed in the pleasure of slurping and sloshing Billy's large erection. Billy's breathing intensified and with his moans growing louder, he yelled for John to stop. "I'm going to cum," he shouted. But it was already too late and he arched his back as he climaxed. John did not hesitate, even for a moment, and eagerly swallowed everything that Billy put out.

"Oh God, Oh God," Billy said breathlessly.

"Oh, yes, oh yes." John looked up with a large smile on his face.

"Come here," Billy grabbed his face and brought him up to kiss him again. "You know what you are doing!"

"I must confess, you are not my first," John replied with an impish grin.

"Then do you know what I want now?" Billy said.

"No."

"I want you to fuck me. Fulfill my dream. Please."

John raised Billy's legs and put them on his shoulders. He spit into his hand twice and rubbed the saliva over his penis and slowly moved to push it into the open and eager hole. Billy winced briefly, but with a firm hand on John's butt, pulled him forward. It did not take long for John to breathe hard, and, with almost a sob, lurch forward to fall onto Billy.

They lay still on top of each other for several minutes. John pulled himself up.

"Come on, time for a quick swim."

The sun was now in full set, the sky a rosy pink, which was reflected in the water. They washed themselves off, gave each other another kiss and held each other as they watched the giant red bulb sink into the horizon.

As it started to get dark, they left the water and got

back to their towels. They dressed silently and packed their bags.

Finally, Billy grabbed John by the arm. "So, now what?" he asked.

"I don't know. I don't care. We'll figure it out. I just know that I love you," John replied, looking deep into Billy's eyes.

"I love you too."

9

Billy crawled into his bed at the rectory and looked at the clock. It was nearly 2 a.m. His room, his bed, the rectory, all were familiar yet everything felt strange and out of place. The flight from Hawai'i had been exhausting. Delayed by nearly three hours due to weather and head winds, Billy had sat next to John during the flight with Becca across the aisle. They barely talked during the nine hours they were together. Billy tried to sleep but couldn't. He was acutely aware of the sexual tension between them and an awkwardness it seemed they both felt, which caused each to be very careful not to touch the other in any way. Billy worried that every glance toward John would reveal his longing for him and so he had deliberately looked out the window most of the flight. Yet, he was annoyed every time he did look toward John and Becca as they had their noses buried in a novel, their way to make the time pass.

As he lay in bed, he pulled his blanket over his head. He had set his alarm for 7:30 as Red had left a note asking him to say the morning Mass. He slept fitfully. His only dream was of swimming among the fish in Hawai'i but with a constant fear that a shark might appear at any moment. The shark never appeared; there was just the fear.

After saying Mass, he ate a quick breakfast and set out for the one person he trusted enough to speak honestly with, Sister Jane. He had carefully avoided any encounter with Red. Billy arrived at New Hope Recovery House just as a yoga class was breaking up. He looked around and didn't see Sister Jane. He asked Melinda, a young volunteer yoga instructor, where she might be.

"Probably in hiding, I think upstairs," she answered pointing skyward.

"Hiding? What's happened?" Billy asked.

"You haven't heard?" Melinda pulled Billy into a corner, away from the small group that was folding up their mats. "Two days ago Johnny Oldshoes collapsed during an AA meeting. He stopped breathing. He seemed dead for sure. Sister Jane prayed over him, said the prayers of anointing, you know for the forgiveness of sins, and suddenly he came back to life. He sat up and starting talking about a white light that was taking him away, that he heard Sister's voice and knew God wanted him to come back to her. Well, the whole group heard it and praised God that Sister Jane had healed him. It didn't take one day for the whole Mission District to know about it. People started coming around asking for Sister to pray over them, or their sick kid or their grandmother. Pretty soon there was a line out the door. It totally freaked poor Sister out, so she has sort of gone into hiding. We tell everybody she's not here, that she's on a retreat. Actually she's upstairs in her room. I'm sure she'd like to see you."

"Oh my, that's quite a story. It's on the left on the third floor at the end of the hallway, right?"

"Yes. Just knock gently and tell her who you are," Melinda answered, waving a short goodbye.

Billy gently knocked several times before he heard a faint voice answer, "Yes?"

"Sister, it's Father Billy. I'm sorry to bother you, but can I please talk with you? It's kind of an emergency."

The door opened and Billy stepped into a darkened room.

"Come in, Billy. I'm not quite myself, but perhaps it would do me some good to talk too."

Billy noticed dark lines under Sister Jane's eyes. Her short hair was slightly mussed as if it hadn't been combed in several days. She was wearing jeans, a T-shirt and no shoes.

"I have a kettle, do you want a cup of tea?" she asked.

"Yes, that would be good." He headed toward a table in front of a large window and sat down. "I hear you have had some excitement around here."

"You could say that. I don't know what to make of it." He sat in silence as the kettle boiled and Jane poured two cups of tea. "Honey?" she asked, setting the cups down on the table.

"No, thank you." A few more minutes passed without either saying a word.

"You said something about an emergency. What's up?"

Billy stared out the window. He tried to think of how to start speaking about Hawai'i and the week that had changed his life. He was afraid to turn his head and look at Sister Jane because he didn't know whether he might burst into tears or a wild, exuberant laugh. Finally he turned and saw her questioning yet accepting eyes upon him. "I don't know where to begin. I'm so confused. I'm scared to death but I'm overjoyed and happy. I'm ashamed and proud. I might just pop out of my skin. I'm a mess."

"Hmm. It sounds to me like you are in love."

"My God! How did you know?" Billy's eyes opened wide with surprise and relief.

Jane smiled. "It was a guess, but it might be that I've been there and I remember the feeling. So take a deep breath and tell me the details."

"I think I told you that Al Pevehaus had introduced me to a wealthy couple in Pacific Heights who are going to fund this survey on the Latino community. Well, they invited me to take a vacation with them in Hawai'i, all expenses paid. So I went. It was an experience like nothing else I have ever had. We went to Kauai, which is so beautiful I can't begin to describe it. All week long, John, the husband and I did one fun, exciting and new activity after another. Snorkeling, hiking, sailing, kayaking, biking. You name it, we did it. It was so much fun. I've never had such fun in my life. No worries, no problems. Just fun. But we talked too. I mean we really got to know each other. We became close. And now I am totally in love with him. I can't stop thinking about him. I don't know what to do. I mean, he's married. I'm a priest. He's rich, I'm poor. Oh God, what do I do?" Billy finally paused to take a breath.

"Well, people often have feelings for each other after a week in paradise. Does he know how you feel about him?" she asked with slight chuckle and a wide grin.

"Yes, I think he does."

"Did you tell him?"

"Yes."

"How did he respond?"

Billy looked at Jane and didn't say anything.

"It's okay, Billy, you can tell me," she said, nodding gently.

"First, he kissed me." Billy looked down at the table. "Then we made love."

"How wonderful!"

Billy looked up at Jane in surprise and confusion. "Wonderful? Isn't it horrible? I can't tell you how much guilt I feel. I mean we broke every rule in the book. I broke my promise of celibacy, I had sex with a man, I betrayed Becca, his wife. God knows what sins I have led John into. I've put him into a terrible bind. I feel so ashamed. But I can't wait to see him again. I want to be with him every minute. My life is ruined, but I feel so unbelievably happy. What am I going to do?" Billy jumped up from the table, threw his hands into the air and began to pace the room.

"First, you are going to calm down. Sit."

Billy just stared at her.

Jane let out a long and deep sigh. "You are in love, that is all. Everything you did was out of love. You are so human. It's how God made us. It's what we are supposed to do, love another human being. It will sort itself out. Don't worry. It will be painful, though. I've had the same experience as you. I fell in love with a married woman, a mother of three small children, and she with me. I remember feeling all the things you are speaking about. It's wonderful and horrible all at the same time."

Billy sat.

"So, was this your first time?" Jane asked.

"Well, yes and no. I mean it was the first time with John, but I am not a virgin. But I have never been in love like this. I had an affair in high school with an older man, a priest. And in college I had a few experiences, which were pretty unsatisfying, but I have been celibate since then. I have been very careful never to get emotionally involved with anyone. I mean this took me totally by surprise. We were just having so much fun, and he was so wonderful to me, and it was so beautiful in Hawai'i. I don't think he realized what was happening either because he didn't know what to do and I think he is as totally freaked out as I am. He could barely look at me on the flight back."

"Okay. What can I do to help?"

"Just listen to me. I had to tell someone. I don't have anyone I really trust. What should I do next? Should I contact him? Should I wait for him to contact me? I thought maybe I should go on a retreat to see if I can get over this or ask for a transfer, someplace far away. But I don't want to lose him; he is such a wonderful man. I want to be with him." Billy sat back in the chair, feeling embarrassed as he heard himself sound like a love sick teenager.

"My advice is first to pray. We can pray together that God will be with you on this journey to discover what His will is for you. He has brought you two together and created a beautiful love between you. It is for a reason. Perhaps it is so that you can break out of your self-imposed emotional isolation and learn to love with more abandon. Perhaps it is to decide if celibate priesthood is right for you. Perhaps it is for John to decide who he really is and if he should stay in his marriage. I don't know. But things happen in our lives for a reason, and we must pray to discern the reasons and learn from them. With this kind of prayer, you have to learn to sit with a lot of feelings, a lot of conflicting feelings, which seem like torture some times. You should not make any rash decisions or actions." Jane reached out and held Billy's hand. "This is a wonderful moment in your life. Surrender to it. God is leading you and sometimes it is through your gonads, so expect to be surprised."

"What happened to you?" Billy asked with a shy smile.

"Oh, I met this wonderful woman a number of years ago when I was in grad school. I had sort of burnt out working with migrant laborers and Mother Superior thought I needed a change of scenery, so she sent me back to school to get a Masters. Marge, that's her name, and I started having a coffee after class, just chatting. Then we had dinner, talked on the phone all the time and finally after six months took a weekend trip to Tahoe. She had such a great sense of humor. She made me laugh so, and she was so understanding and gentle. I'd never been with such a sweet, tender woman. All the women in my family are tough, cynical and bitter. Well, it came time for bed on the first night and I wanted to give her a quick good night kiss, but she kissed me back tenderly and lovingly. So I kissed her again, and well, one thing led to another. I realized then that I was completely in love with her and nothing mattered more than being with her. We gave ourselves to each other the whole weekend. I was never in such pain as when we had to go back to our lives. I didn't want that weekend to ever end."

"What happened?"

"We kept up our relationship in secret until the end of the academic year, seeing each other and talking every day, stealing away time together to make love on some weekends or evenings. In the end, she decided not to leave her husband and so broke it off. She dropped out of school, her husband got transferred and I haven't heard from her in over ten years.

I was crushed. I didn't know what to do with my life. Should I stay or leave? Find another woman to love? I prayed and prayed. Then one day at Mass, I just had this overwhelming experience that God had plans for me. I felt so very loved by Him. I felt that the way to be healed was to work with the sickest and the neediest people I could find. So, here I am. But I still miss Meg and I think of her every day. And I wouldn't trade our time together for anything."

"Thank you for sharing that, Sister. I'm not sure it makes me feel any better. I don't think I could bear it if John just cut me off, though it might make my life easier," Billy sighed. He looked at Jane and said sadly, "It does feel better though, that I have told someone."

"Come talk to me any time. Keep praying. Let God speak to your heart and your head and things will get clearer over time. In the meantime, enjoy it, embrace it and for heaven's sake don't run from it. Remember, love is a gift."

"Speaking of gifts," Billy asked, "Tell me what happened here last week!"

"Oh God, I don't know. We were right in the middle of an AA meeting when old Johnny Oldshoes starting speaking. He said he had something important to say, then he stood up and dropped dead. He just collapsed and lay lifeless on the floor. Someone called 911. I tried a little CPR but I couldn't detect any breathing or a pulse and he turned gray. I just felt moved to pray over him, so I started to say some of the prayers for the dying. I anointed his eyes with spit, then his ears and lips. I picked up his hands and made the sign of the cross in the palms, then suddenly he started to breathe again. His color came back. Then he opened his eyes, sat up and said, 'Thank you Lord'. Well, we got him into a chair and he told me that God wanted him to come back here and give me a message."

Sister Jane paused and looked away.

"What was the message?"

"That He wants me to heal with love."

"What do you think that means?" Billy asked, looking confused.

"I don't know. Love is always healing and that is what I have been trying to do all these years. So, am I to just continue what I'm doing? I don't think I need a special message to keep doing that. Or does it mean something else? Anyway, it didn't take long before people starting talking like I had a special healing power and wanted me to lay hands on them. Maria Pescado brought her sick daughter in. What was I going to do? I prayed over her and touched her chest and Maria said that she was immediately a lot better. There was a line down the street by evening. I do not want to be some celebrity faith healer. I think people are imagining all kinds of things. It just got out of hand, so I decided to go into hiding for a few days. Let things calm down. This instant healing stuff isn't real. Real healing comes from recovery and that takes a long time."

"I see your point. But do you think you really brought Johnny Oldshoes back to life?" Billy asked.

"I didn't do anything. If he came back from wherever he was, God did it. Not me. I'm Jane, remember? Nun, lesbian and a regular human being. Full of my own issues and crap. The last thing I need is for people to be putting me on a pedestal or thinking I can do some kind of magic. It will all blow over, I'm sure. I just need to keep my head down for a while."

"That makes two of us," Billy said getting up to leave. "Thanks for being such a good listener. I'll watch your back and you can keep me from being a crazy man."

"Deal. Take care. Call or come by any time."

10

The faint sound of a siren filtered

slowly into his consciousness. He was jostled back and forth as the ambulance turned a corner. He had a splitting headache and he slowly opened his eyes.

"Just stay still. You are going to be all right. Can you see my fingers? How many am I holding up?"

"Three."

"Good. Can you tell me your name?"

"Where am I? What's going on?"

"You are in an ambulance heading to San Francisco General Hospital. You were knocked out. Someone found you and called 911. Your vitals are okay. Are you in any pain anywhere? Arms, legs, stomach?"

"Just my head."

"Can you raise your left arm? Good. Now your right. Lift your legs. Okay, good."

"Oh my God. I was attacked."

"Yes, but I think you will survive. Now help me with this paperwork. What is your name? You didn't have any identification on you."

"My name." Silence.

"Yes, can you remember your name?"

"Yes of course. But do you have to have my name?"

"I'm afraid so."

"Sylvester Peterson."

"OK, Sylvester. My name is Frank. What's your address?"

"I'm afraid I don't know the street address."

"You don't know where you live?"

"Of course, I do. I live at St. Mary's Cathedral. On Geary Street."

"Okay. Are you a priest or something there?"

"I am the Archbishop of San Francisco."

"OK. Well, I'm not Catholic, Father, so I didn't know. Is there someone we can call when we get to the hospital? Someone who can bring us your health insurance information?"

"Yes. Call Father Cody. He is my secretary and lives at St. Mary's as well. I don't remember the phone number. You can look it up."

"Okay. Well, you just relax, Father. We'll be there shortly and get you right in for some tests to make sure you don't have a concussion or any other serious problems. You've got quite a gash on your forehead but that will heal up nicely."

The Emergency Medical Technician picked up a microphone, "This is AM 2113 calling in. We are bringing in an assault victim with a possible concussion. All vitals indicate normal, no broken bones or other obvious injuries. Says he is the Archbishop of San Francisco, so consider it Priority One."

"Ten Four, 2113. Go to west side entrance."

"He said to notify a Father Cody at St. Mary's Cathedral, unknown phone number. Victim has no identification on him. Notify SFPD. Also tell Father Cody to bring a fresh shirt. The victim is wearing a white shirt that is pretty bloody."

As the Archbishop was wheeled into the emergency room, he was engulfed by a swarm of people, none of whom paid any attention to him as they were all there seeking treatment for themselves. Pushing through the crowd was a priest and a doctor.

"Your Excellency, I am Father Tom Corcoran. I'm the chaplain here. They notified me immediately that you were on your way in. This is Dr. Michael Kenny, the senior clinician on duty and a good Catholic. He will take good care of you."

"Thank you, Father," the Archbishop said, looking around in bewilderment.

An hour later, the Archbishop was sitting up in a chair in a well-furnished private room. Dr. Kenny had determined there was only a small chance of concussion and so had authorized his release. Two police officers entered the room.

"Archbishop, my name is Detective Paul Orlando and this is Sergeant Peter Samanta. We need to ask you a few questions if you feel up to it. Just formalities. It shouldn't take but a couple of minutes."

"Yes, yes, of course. But do we have to do this tonight? I mean, can we do it tomorrow or the next day?

"It's best if we do it now. The sooner after an incident the better. We might have a better chance of catching the guy who did this to you. I promise you it will be quick and easy," the detective said with some insistence.

"What questions do you have?" the Archbishop asked, showing his irritation.

"Do you have any memory of what happened? You were hit from the front, so do you remember what your assailant looked like?"

"I don't. It was dark. I don't remember anything, just waking up in the ambulance."

"Do you remember when you went to the park? The call came in at 10:35 p.m. and the ambulance arrived at the scene at 10:47 and noted that you were unconscious."

"I don't. Maybe 10 o'clock."

"May I ask the Archbishop why you were at the park at night? Were you with anyone?"

"No." The Archbishop stared across the room. After a moments hesitation, he blurted out, "I went to say the rosary. I often go to a park at night to say the rosary. It's quiet and peaceful. I always stay on the paths and in light. I didn't think it would be dangerous."

"Did you drive there?"

"Yes, I parked on the street."

"May I ask why you picked Buena Vista Park?"

"No reason, really. Why do you ask?"

"Well, that park is pretty busy at night. It has a bit of a reputation."

"I don't know. I'm relatively new to San Francisco."

"You said you stayed on the path. The ambulance found you off the path in a clump of bushes. Do you remember anyone luring you into the bushes? Do you remember speaking with anyone?"

"No. I remember passing several people but I did not pay much attention to them and they didn't seem to pay much attention to me. I don't know how I got off the path. Maybe I was dragged," the Archbishop replied with a slight twitch of his eye.

"Could be, but your clothes don't show any sign of being dragged."

"Really Officers, these questions are getting rather tiring. Is there anything else you need to know? I really don't remember much of anything."

"No, I think that is about it, Archbishop. Not much to go on, I'm afraid. The person who called in did not leave a name or number but did call from a cell phone so we can track him down. Thank you for your cooperation." Both officers turned and began to leave.

"One thing, Detective. You said that park had a reputation. What did you mean by that?" the Archbishop asked.

"Well, Sir, it is well known as a haunt for gay men looking for sex. We try to patrol it the best we can but generally it's not a high violent crime area, just a lot of sex in the bushes," the Detective replied, looking closely at the Archbishop all the while trying to suppress a smirk.

"I see. Well, I certainly had no idea about that, I can assure you," the Archbishop sputtered with bravado.

"Of course not, Archbishop. But I would avoid saying the rosary in parks late at night in the future. Particularly that park."

Father Cody drove the Archbishop back to St. Mary's, each maintaining an uncomfortable silence. Then in a burst of words the Archbishop recounted the entire story he had told the police.

"You know what this means, don't you, Father? I have been attacked by a gay thug, some gay activist who probably recognized me and wanted to make me pay for supporting Proposition 8 and leading the fight against gay marriage. There I was, peacefully praying to Our Lady, and I was attacked, unprovoked, by one of those depraved, evil people. I was lucky I wasn't killed or seriously injured!"

"Yes, your Excellency. That may be it, but it could have been just a simple robbery. I mean they did take your wallet," replied Father Cody, trying to calm his passenger down.

"No, no. I didn't take my wallet to the park. That wasn't it. I'm sure I was attacked because I was recognized and someone wanted to deliver a message to me or put an end to me. They want me to stop this fight, but I will not. It is God's will that we fight even harder to preserve the sanctity of holy marriage. We cannot give in to intimidation. Perhaps this is actually a gift from God to stir up good Catholics to defend their Faith and their Archbishop."

Father Cody knew when to acquiesce and not fight the man. "Yes, Archbishop."

"Father, I think I am in danger. There may be further attacks. I want you to do some research and find a security service we can hire. I think I am going to need armed guards from here on out. It's a dangerous world and you never know when some fanatic will decide he must do something violent."

"Yes, Archbishop."

"And another thing. I think we need to do some investigation into our own back yard. There may be some radical gays inside the Church who are plotting as well. After all, Indira Gandhi was assassinated by her own guards inside the Presidential Palace. We can't be too careful." They drove on in silence. "Yes, tonight might just be a sign from God to take some action and redouble our efforts to defend the faith and the Church."

"Yes, Archbishop."

11

Al Pevehaus pressed the doorbell

a second time at 2800 Pacific Street. He was growing impatient, waiting for the door to open. Just as he was about to press a third time, the door finally opened.

"Good afternoon, Monsignor." Pinky said, bowing slightly. "I apologize for your wait. I was in the basement."

"Oh, not a problem Pinky. I was beginning to worry though. You are always so prompt. How was the vacation to Hawai'i? Did you get some time to relax?" Al marched in, trying to sound breezy and unperturbed.

"Yes, we had lovely weather. It was just the Lady of the house and I all day long, so I did get to rest. The Master is in the library," Pinky stated in a low voice.

Al entered the library to find John staring out the back window. "Paddy, how are you?"

"Oh, hello Al," John said turning. "Fine, just fine."

"Well, good. My, you got quite a tan in just a week. You must have been in the sun a lot," Al reached to shake John's hand. "Did Billy run you around a bit?"

"Ah, yes. Billy did. I mean, actually it was the other way around. I gave him a total immersion into the possibilities of outdoor fun in Kauai. We snorkeled, hiked, biked, kayaked, sailed and even just swam. It was a lovely time. Drink?"

"Yes, please. So tell me all about it."

John looked at Al with a stunned expression on his face, then quickly recovered and turned to Pinky. "Two glasses of that new single malt, Pinky, the one that came yesterday."

"Did everything work out all right with Billy? You looked like you'd seen a ghost."

"Oh yes, of course. We had a wonderful time," John said, looking away. He avoided Al's eye.

"Then why the strange look? I know you. Something is up."

John looked around. "Let's take our scotch and go out into the garden." After Pinky arrived with their drinks, they headed out the door to the privacy of the back garden terrace.

"Beautiful day, isn't it?" John said casually.

"Yes, it is. Okay, we are alone now. You can trust me. What happened?" Al said pulling close to John.

"Oh Al. I don't know how to tell you this." John spoke softly yet with an urgency that revealed his high level of anxiety. "I have to talk to someone. It's driving me crazy and I don't know what to do."

"Alright, calm down. Go on, get it out."

"I think I fell in love." John looked skyward, then away from Al, toward the bay.

"With Billy?"

"Yes."

"Is that all?! Well, I don't blame you. I did too, once upon a time, though he was much younger," Al replied, suddenly realizing how much he was revealing in just a few, short sentences.

John glared at Al with a mixture of incredulity, jealousy and anger. Then getting control of himself, he again turned away. "I don't see how you can make light of what I just said."

Al, sorting out all the feelings that had just been projected at him, pulled back. "I wasn't making light of it John. I'm sorry. This must be very confusing for you. Sit down. Tell me everything."

"I don't know that I can sit. It is confusing and upsetting. Al, I can't stop thinking of him. In just a short time, I felt so close to him. He is so beautiful, I mean, handsome. His exuberance and vitality, his warmth and wonder at everything. He's all man, but he can be so tender too. I've never felt so alive."

"Yes, he is wonderful," Al replied, careful not to bring himself back into the conversation.

John looked down suddenly, with a desperately sad expression. "What am I to do? I'm a married man. He's a priest. I have two sons not much younger than him. I can't stop thinking of him and want to be with him all the time, yet I'm terrified to see him again. I don't know what I would do if I saw him again, kiss him or run? I'm so miserable."

"Oh John. I'm so sorry for your pain."

There was a few minutes of silence between them. John turned and asked, "What did you mean "you did too'?"

Al knew this comment was bound to come back to him. "Well, when Billy was in high school, I sort of fell in love with him. It was a long time ago. We are long over it. It was years and years ago."

"He mentioned that he had once loved another man. That must have been you. I never suspected. Have there been others?"

Al sighed, "There have been others. Not many, but others."

"This is the first time I have ever fallen in love with a man. I must confess that I have always been attracted to men, I mean, in some physical way, but I have never let it go beyond fantasy. I love Becca. We have a great life together. I would never hurt her. I just don't know how this happened. It just crept up on me and suddenly, I was kissing him. And it was magic."

"Does Becca know? Have you talked with her about this?"

"No. No. I don't think she suspects anything. No, I haven't told her. I don't know how. I don't know what to say. I don't know what I want. I don't know what Billy wants or how he feels since we've come back. You are the first and only person I have spoken to about this. I was hoping you could give me some advice. What should I do?"

"Well, my advice for the moment is to just keep quiet and let your feelings sort out. If you like I will talk with Billy. He is probably as confused as you. Perhaps after a week or two, you guys can meet and figure how you both can deal with this new infatuation. We are all going to have to work together too, I mean on the survey project. You're sure no one knows about this but you two?"

"Hmmm. Well, there is always Pinky. He seems to always know everything. He could probably tell you whether I had a good shit this morning, so he may suspect something about Billy and me. But he is completely discrete. He won't say anything. At least, I don't think he would," John replied, looking back toward to the door to the library.

"Ah, the joys and tribulations of domestic servants," Al said with a chuckle. "I never know what he's thinking myself and I've known him for twenty years."

"You aren't the only one. But I do trust him. He's very loyal."

"So what do you want me to do Paddy?"

"I don't know. I don't know that I want to get you in the middle of this. Am I crazy or what? Why am I even in this situation?" John jumped up out of his chair and began to pace.

"Calm down, it will be okay," Al said. Inwardly, he was trying to sort out his own emotional reaction to this surprising news. He empathized with John and felt a little sorry for his mental turmoil, but deeper there was a pang of jealousy as well. Even though the affair with Billy had ended years before, he didn't feel the sexual pull that he once felt for Billy when he was a young teenager. Billy was still one of the loves of Al's sordid life and he felt some sense of ownership over him. Billy had become a sort of "priestly son" to him. He felt very unsure about how he might approach Billy with this subject but he was sure that he had a wide array of conflicting feelings.

Suddenly Pinky appeared without a sound. "May I get you anything?" he asked.

"Yes, Pinky, thank you. Another Al? The same?"

"Sure."

As Pinky left, John gave Al a stare. "Perhaps we should talk about this another time," John said in a whisper. "But I guess it would be helpful to me if you spoke with him. I'm so afraid of making a fool of myself."

"Alright, Paddy. I'll get back to you." They finished their second drink over small talk and Al departed.

Al wasn't sure how he going to approach Billy but he knew he had to spend some time thinking about it before he did. First, he needed another drink. He drove straight to the rectory.

Feigning a touch of the flu, he cancelled plans for dinner with another Pac Heights couple he was wooing for some money. He sat in the chair in his bedroom and proceeded to begin some serious drinking. It was 3:30 in the afternoon and he was hoping for a near stupor before 5, the sooner the better to numb the feelings that kept raging about Billy and Paddy. He was deeply jealous, not that they were having sex but that they were in love.

It had been too many years since he had been in love. In fact, the truth was he had not been in love since he and Billy first met nearly fifteen years ago, when those big, sweet brown eyes had fluttered at him the first time in the sophomore religion class that he was teaching. Billy's earnest, adoring interest in everything Al said, along with a quick dimpled smile had captured Al's immediate attention. It had not taken long before he was completely bewitched and then hopelessly in love with him.

He slouched further into his chair after the fourth scotch and let himself remember those wonderful feelings of dizziness, of bodily craving, a total loss of mental will and control, of a weightlessness that seemed like floating on a cloud, all coupled with the most extreme anxiety that his desires might not be reciprocated, that he would be rejected. To be newly in love was the most exhilarating of all feelings and yet also the most exquisitely painful at the same time. As his reverie deepened, so did the curse of feeling sorry for himself. Slowly, it engulfed him. Weepy tears of self-pity began to trickle down his cheeks. Then came the all too familiar mental messages: "Life is over. There is nothing left but pain and suffering. I'm old, fat, ugly, undesirable and sad."

He took another large gulp from his drink. He closed his eyes, hoping that he would drift into a dull sleep, which had nearly overtaken him when his phone beeped that he had a text message. Only slightly aroused, he muttered, "Fuck it", closed his eyes and did not reach for the phone. A second beep annoyed him enough that he grabbed the phone just to see who was pestering him. It was Jake, the last rent boy he had indulged.

"Hey handsome. What's up? Haven't heard from you."

Since when did rent boys solicit? The world was changing. "He must need to pay the rent," Al thought. Yet, maybe Jake had truly liked him. Maybe Jake missed him. Maybe Jake was lonely too. So he needed some money, maybe it was more than that. He texted back, "Been busy. What's up with you?"

"Me 2. Nothing going 2night and thought of you. Want to have some fun?"

"Maybe."

"Real horny. Did I say that?"

"Oh."

"You got plans?"

"No."

"Well?"

Al thought for a minute. The last time wasn't that great. Jake was cute all right, but there wasn't much connection. He had seemed in a hurry. But maybe tonight would be different. Besides, Al needed a little company, with someone who wanted him. He texted, "OK. I want to have dinner first. With you."

"Really?"

"Yes. I'll pay of course."

"Well, I gotta eat. Where?"

"Catch, Castro and Market. 7."

"K. What about after?"

"We'll see about after. Your place free?"

"Always available. Not always free. Lol."

"Yes, I remember. See you at 7"

"K."

Al sat back and looked around his room. It was getting dark. "I've got to get cleaned up. I have a date," he mused, half-pleased with himself. The self-pity had lifted, as had the thoughts of Billy and Paddy. He was on the make again. "Who knows. I might get lucky," he muttered half aloud.

It was nearly 7:20 before Al saw Jake enter the restaurant. He looked at his watch in annoyance as Jake approached the table.

"Sorry man, I got delayed. Muni sucks you know." Jake sat down without looking at Al. "I've never done this before. I mean, had dinner with a customer. It's kinda weird."

"Well, there isn't much to it. Look at the menu, order some food and we'll make small talk while we eat. I just didn't want to be alone tonight, that's all."

"Okay. I'll have the steak. And how about a mojito?"

"Sure. Help yourself," Al replied. The waiter came and they ordered.

"My name is Al by the way. And you might as well know, I'm a priest."

"No shit. A Catholic priest?"

"Yes. Can I trust you with that information?"

"Your secret's good with me, man. I don't care. My job is to be discrete."

"Good. Are you Catholic?" Al asked, hoping the answer would be "No."

"No. I'm nothing. Wasn't raised nothing. Had a single mom who has her problems. No time for church and stuff," Jake said with a slight smirk. "So is that why you find guys like me? I mean, priests aren't supposed to have sex at all, right?"

"Yeah, that's right. Hasn't worked out very well for me though," Al said fingering his glass of wine.

"Can't think how it would work out for anybody. Mind if I ask you a personal question?" Jake looked up skittishly at Al.

"Okay."

"How old are you?"

"I'm 67. Why do you ask?"

"Just wondering. I've been with a lot of older guys. I like 'em."

"How old are you?" Al asked.

"Usually I answer that by asking, "How old do you want me to be?" I mean, some guys want me to be sixteen, other guys want me to be legal, but most guys don't want to know the truth," Jake answered straightforwardly.

"How old are you really?"

"Twenty-three."

"You look a lot younger."

"Yeah."

"How's the mojito? Want another?"

"No, I'm doin' Okay. So Al, can I use your name? Why did you want to have dinner. You seem kind of down," Jake asked, looking sympathetically at Al.

"Well, to be honest, I just found out one of my best friends is in love with my former boyfriend and it's driving me nuts. I wanted to be with a cute guy who might pretend he likes me. Does that answer your question?" Al replied with a hint of aggression.

"Shit! That hurts. How long since you guys broke up?"

"Ten years, maybe longer."

"Whoa, that's a while. You still have lots of feelings for the guy though. I'm sorry." Jake put his hand on Al's.

"Yeah, I do. Thanks, that's sweet of you."

"Listen, after dinner come back to my place and I'll make you forget about this guy, at least for a while. I'll take extra good care of you."

"Yeah, I feel like I need a little extra care," Al said lifting his hand and smiling slightly at Jake.

"My last boyfriend fucking left in the middle of the night six months ago and robbed me of five thousand dollars cash, all my savings. Probably used it to pay off his dealer. The fucker was a total tweeker but he had a line of bullshit a mile long. He was a great fuck. So stupid of me. I ignored all the screaming red flags and let him move in with me. I was so pissed. But what hurt more was that I loved the guy. He was so hot. I thought he love me too. We had plans. Ha! The shit!"

Al watched as Jake's features had reddened. With a curled upper lip, his eyes opened wide, his pupils dilated and his pointed tongue spit out the words. He could feel the passion and anger rising from the thin, boyish, shaggy blond who moments before had seemed so passive and sweet. He liked that Jake was showing him some real emotion, telling him a real hurt from his past and not just playing the detached rent-boy.

"How old was he?" Al asked.

"Forty-five."

Al thought to himself, "So does he like older guys? Maybe there is a chance with me?" He said to the rent boy, "That sounds awful. I'm sorry. By the way, what's your real name? I mean, is it Jake?"

"No."

"So, what is it?"

"You promise not to laugh?"

"I promise."

"Cloud."

"Cloud? You mean like in the cloud in the sky?" Al asked, trying very hard not smile in any way.

"Yeah. Hippy mother. Bitch." He paused, "Jake is a lot hotter, don't ya think?"

"Cloud is pretty exotic though for a certain clientele."

"Yeah, well, let's keep it to Jake, OK?"

"Sure, but thanks for being honest with me," he said looking Jake in the eye.

"What's Al stand for?"

"Alvin."

"Ooo, you should stick with Al."

"I agree. How's the steak?"

"Great. These potatoes are awesome. Want a taste?" Jake asked, lifting his fork with a potato on it. Al opened his mouth and ate it.

"Yummy." He loved the fact that they were acting like they were on a date, sharing food. "Want a bite of my fish?"

"Sure." Jake smiled at Al with a dreamy look in his eye, like he was enjoying the whole date-like experience too. "I like the ginger flavor."

They chatted about their favorite foods and Al regaled

Jake about a few memorable dishes he had in Rome as they finished their dinner.

"So, you were in the Vatican. I mean, did you ever meet the new Pope or anything?" Jake asked a bit wide-eyed.

"As a matter of fact I did have a private meeting with him," Al answered, trying not to think about the circumstances of that infamous meeting that ended his career.

"Whoa. He is some dude," Jake remarked carelessly.

"Yes, he is. Have you met anyone famous?"

"I went to a Springsteen concert once. I guess that doesn't quite count for meeting him," Jake answered unassumingly. "Maybe you are most famous person I have met so far. I mean you met the Pope and he's somebody."

Al smiled. He was touched. "That's sweet. Let me pay the check and we can head back to your place. OK?"

"Sure man."

Al signed the credit card slip and surreptitiously slipped two Viagra pills into his mouth and drank some water.

As they headed back to the Tenderloin, Al drove a bit aggressively, trying to impress Jake with his new clerical-jet black Porsche. As he glanced sideways, Jake seemed more frightened than impressed, which gave Al a firm sense of being in control. Inside Jake's neat studio, Al reached over and pulled Jake to him for a kiss. Jake responded by throwing his arms around Al's head and giving him a deep, long wet kiss.

"Let's get these clothes off," Jake said with a smile.

Lying under the sheets of his bed, Jake set about to make Al feel very pampered, spending lots of time with kisses, caresses and a few gentle licks to his ears. He alternated between being passive, letting Al kiss and touch him as he wanted, then turn more aggressive and move over Al's body with a hunger and desire that reacted with enjoyment each time Al responded with pleasure.

"Turn over. I'll give you a little massage," Jake said quietly.

"That would be nice."

Jake's hands were firm but gentle. Al groaned a few times as he felt the stress of his shoulders and back releasing and noticed that the effects of the Viagra were beginning to work on his growing erection. As Jake massaged his way down to the gluts, Al felt the warmth of a gentle lick at his butthole, then a cooling breathy breeze.

"Oh you sweet nasty boy," he said with a small chuckle.

"Sshhh. Relax and enjoy."

Jake continued to rub and lick and kiss Al in a way that he could never remember experiencing before. He felt like he was truly being made love to with such tenderness that it almost made him weep.

"Turn over. Hmmm, it seems you liked all that," Jake said as he eyed Al's erection. Immediately lowering his head, he engulfed Al with his mouth, gently massaging his scrotum.

"Oh my God, you have a magic tongue." His excitement growing, he arched his back. "Oh God. Wait, wait, not too much, not too fast. I want to fuck you!" Al blurted out, surprising himself.

"With pleasure, my sweet," Jake replied. He rolled over on his back, spread his legs and raised them.

Al moved quickly to lay on top of him. He was feeling like the twenty-year old stud of his past and wanted to lose none of the momentum of the moment. As he entered him, Jake pulled Al's head down to his and gave him a passionate kiss. With just two minutes of pumping and panting, Al cried out as he released his load inside Jake, sweat and tears together dripping down his cheek. "Oh my God. Oh my God," Al muttered as he collapsed onto Jake's chest.

"Yes, my, what a God you are. And all man," Jake said quietly into his ear. Al lay with his head on Jake's chest, gently kissing his nipple as he sought to catch his breath and recover his emotions.

"Do you want to cum?" Al asked looking up into Jake's smiling face.

"Oh I came when you did. I'm fine. Just rest," he replied running his hands through Al's hair. "Feel a bit better?"

"Oh yes, yes. Thank you so much."

After five minutes, Al sat up. "Well, I guess I need to go, don't I?"

"No hurry. Take your time."

Al slowly got off the bed, gathered his clothes and went to the bathroom. As he dressed, he remembered that he had skipped putting on a condom, reflected a minute and then dismissed any thought of danger. What was the chance? None really, he had been the top.

Emerging from the bathroom, he found Jake in a Japanese bathrobe. He placed eight one hundred dollar bills on the side table, all the money he had brought with him. Jake pretended to pay no attention. Al approached Jake and grabbed him for a hug.

Jake gave Al a final, longish kiss. "I like you. Let's do this again. You shouldn't feel so sad."

"Yes, me too," Al replied starting get a little emotional. He stopped himself. "Do you like Japanese?" Al asked touching Jake's cheek.

"Love it!"

12

Billy left Jane and drove to Ocean Beach. He had to think and he had to pray and in his mind there was no place more private or anonymous. He parked his car in the grey fog that enshrouded the parking lot. He put on his parka and taking off his shoes got out of the car and headed for the water. It was a typical summer day in San Francisco, a damp mid-50s temperature, fog about a hundred feet off the ground and a slight breeze that made it feel ten degrees cooler. There being no sun, there were no bathers, just a few hearty souls walking their dogs on a huge expansive beach that ran about five miles to his left. The noise of the crashing waves blocked out any other sounds. Billy walked as if he were in a cocoon of solitude and silence.

As he stepped along the hardened sand close to the water, he was careful not to get his feet wet as the ocean was even colder than the windy fog. He tried to pray, saying the traditional Our Father and Hail Mary, but they seemed stale and ineffective. "What am I to do?" were the only words that repeatedly came to him. He began to say them aloud, over and over like a mantra, first softly then louder as no one was around to hear him. After ten minutes he was exhausted and his mouth dry. He moved away from the water, twenty feet up the beach and threw himself down in the sand and lay staring up at the grey abyss. Suddenly he shouted out "Help me Lord! I'm going crazy!" He waited for an answer but there was no sound except the crashing of the waves. He closed his eyes and just lay for another ten minutes. Finally, beginning to relax, he slowly drifted off into semi-conscious nap.

He felt the cold wet skin brush up against his cheek and he jerked awake with a gasp, startling and scaring a beautiful golden retriever that had been sniffing him out. The dog jumped two feet and looked eagerly back at him. "Oh, hello boy. Sorry to scare you. Come here." Billy held out his hand to the dog. "Come here. I won't hurt you." Petting him as he moved close to Billy, his tail was wagging energetically. Billy spoke sweetly, "It's okay. You scared me too. Good boy."

"Sam. Come here and leave that man alone!" a lady fifty feet away call out. The dog turned his head and ran to his master, obedient to the call.

"Bye Sam," Billy said with a trace of sorrow.

He got to his feet, brushed himself off and began to walk back toward his car. His feet tingled as if were they completely frozen. He recalled his cry for help and his mind wandered back to the encounter with Sam. He pondered, "Were those words meant for me? *Leave that man alone.* Was that God answering me?" He recalled how the dog instantly obeyed and ran back to the woman. "Does God want me to return to Him, turn and run just like Sam? Run from John, run from love, run from sex and head directly to the straight and narrow path the Church expects of me? Is that what God expects? Is that what God wants me to do, *right now?!* Maybe those are my marching orders," he thought with a growing conviction.

Billy tied his shoes and turned on the engine of the car. He set the heater to full blast and aimed it at his feet. It was approaching four in the afternoon. He was seized with the need to see John and tell him what God had ordered him to do. He couldn't go on another day with this stress and pain. *He had his orders; he must execute them.* He pulled his car out of the parking lot and headed for 2800 Pacific Avenue.

No sooner had he touched the doorbell, the door opened.

"Good afternoon, Father," Pinky said without emotion.

"Oh, hello Pinky. Is either John or Becca at home?"

"I'm afraid the Madam is out for the afternoon but the Master is here. Please come in," Pinky smiled slightly and opened the door wider. "You just missed the Monsignor, he left a little over an hour ago."

"Did he?"

"Yes. You may wait in the library."

Billy sat down in the wide, book-lined room, trying to breathe deeply as his anxiety rose to a peak that made him dizzy.

John burst through the door. "Hi! Pinky said you were here. How are you?"

Billy was about to speak when he noticed that Pinky was not far behind John. He looked from John to Pinky and didn't open his mouth. John turned around to see what he was looking at.

"Would you like something to drink Billy?" John asked,

turning back.

"No. I'm fine. I just stopped by to say and Hi and chat for a minute," Billy replied.

"Okay, I'm good as well, Pinky. That is all," he said in a slight, dismissive manner.

"Please ring if you need something," Pinky replied and left closing the door quietly behind him.

"So. How are you?" John asked again, moving closer to Billy.

"I'm... I'm terrible!" Billy burst out.

"I'm so sorry. I'm miserable as well. I miss you so much. It's wonderful to see you," John replied, moving closer still.

Billy's eyes welled up with tears.

John grabbed him in a lunge that instantly turned into an embrace and a deeply passionate kiss. "Oh God, I can't help it."

Billy did not resist but rather melted into John's arms and returned the kiss, tears now streaming down his cheeks.

"Why are you crying?" John asked, "Are you happy or sad?"

"Oh, I don't know. I'm a mess," Billy said wiping his eyes with the back of his hand.

"I am too. But it is so wonderful to be with you and hold you in my arms right now. I don't want to think about anything else," John said, leaning in and gently giving him another kiss. "I'm so sorry I was cold during the plane ride back. I just didn't know how to act around you with the whole family there. I hope you didn't think I stopped caring."

"I didn't know what to think. I came here to tell you that I must never see you again, but now I don't want to ever leave you again. I'm so confused. It's torture," Billy said gripping John's arms. They fell into a tight embrace.

"All right. Sit down. Let's calm down and talk about this," John said softly in Billy's ear. They sat on the leather couch facing each other. Looking deeply into each other's eyes, John spoke first, "What's our situation? We deeply care about each other and have become very emotionally attached, but neither of us is free. We have other obligations. We don't want to hurt anyone," he paused, looked down and then up, "But I am totally in love with you and don't want to give that up. I'm sorry, but I'm being so selfish." John reached over and touched Billy's face, drying up a long tear with his thumb. "I understand, it is a terrible conflict for you too. But you know, lots of your brother priests have lovers. Love makes them better priests," John replied, not sure where he got that argument but it sounded good.

"You sound like Sister Jane," Billy replied smiling.

"Who's Sister Jane?"

"She's a nun I talked to about this. She's very special, very holy and really understands these things. I talked with her this morning."

"What did she say?"

"She said this was all God's doing and that I should listen and pay attention to it, and pray about it. That it was all good. Love is always good; it teaches us, even if it's painful," Billy replied. He sounded like he didn't actually believed what he was saying.

"She does sound holy. You are lucky to have someone you can trust to talk with. Speaking of which I must tell you that I confessed our situation to Al Pevehaus a few hours ago, so he knows," John said turning his gaze out the window. "I hope I didn't betray your confidence."

Billy sat back. "Al, huh. Well, I don't entirely trust him. We go way back and he hasn't always been very nice to me, to put it mildly. I know you guys have been friends for years too, but you should be careful with him," Billy said, concerned.

"Yes, he mentioned something about you and him when you were in high school. I'm sorry, I didn't know. I thought you and he were just friends."

"We are. We are long over that bit of history. I'm just saying, be careful what you tell him." Billy paused, "What about Becca?"

"I haven't said anything to her. I don't know what to tell her. Maybe she senses something is up but she's so wrapped up in her own life these days, I mean, she seems to be on every charity committee in the city and is always out. To be honest, I haven't thought much about her because I can't take my mind off you!"

"So, what are we going to do?" Billy asked with a shrug of exasperation.

"When can you can get away for a day or so? I would like to go down the coast, walk on the beach and talk this out. Figure some way we can be in each other's lives, get to know each other better, look at our alternatives, maybe even pray about it. But don't run away from me. Don't disappear," John said holding Billy's shoulders, his own eyes now welling up. They kissed with desperation.

"OK. Thursday is my day off. Let's go somewhere this Thursday. I'm free after the 8 a.m. mass," Billy said standing up. There was a slight rustle at the door.

Outside the library, Mrs. Aquino, the housekeeper, came around the corner into the hallway with a mop in her hand. She was startled to see Pinky pressed to the library door. "Mr. Pinky, what are you doing?"

Pinky, taken by surprise, pushed himself away from the

door with a jerk. "I thought I heard the Master calling me but I wasn't sure. That's all," he said, walking away with haste.

However, Mrs. Aquino noted that she had never before seen Pinky with a beet red color on his face and a look of complete rage. She went about her mopping, but she knew he was very upset, probably and thankfully not with her.

13

Sister Jane left her upper room
retreat under the cover of darkness, catching a cab to the San
Francisco Airport at 5 o'clock in the morning. She had a 6:30
a.m. flight to Philadelphia to place her entire dilemma in the
hands of one of the few people she trusted completely, the
Superior General of the Social Services Sisters, Sister Martha. They had been in the novitiate together twenty-five years
ago. They had a close friendship from then on, though in the
early days "particular friendships" were greatly discouraged.
Fifteen years back, they had served three years together at an
Indian Mission in South Dakota and formed a deep spiritual
bond, praying together every day and recounting their trials,
disappointments and occasional successes over the evening
meal.

Sister Martha had been elected Superior General three
years ago amid an investigation by the U.S. Bishop's Confer-

ence and the Vatican Congregation for the Religious due to complaints from conservatives. Many worried that American nuns were too focused on fighting poverty, immersing themselves in curing the social ills of the poor and generally supporting liberal feminist and even lesbian causes, all the while ignoring the more important need to fight gay marriage, abortion and the rampant use of birth control by the lax general population of Catholics. Sister Martha's deep spirituality, great patience and strong willpower, laced with an unfailing sweetness, had seemed the perfect combination to endure the onslaught of the investigation, accusation and innuendo by these elderly, angry and threatened white men. It was thought that her Ph.D. in Child Development would give her an insight as well as intellectual heft in the coming battles.

Jane's early arrival allowed her to get to the Mother House in time for Vespers with the five other sisters living there. The Mother House was located in a hundred year old, graffiti covered convent in a downtrodden neighborhood of East Philly. After prayers and a simple meal, Sister Martha motioned to Jane to follow her upstairs.

Once inside Sister Martha's spacious room, she turned and embraced Sister Jane with a warm hug and a sweet kiss on the cheek.

"Oh Jane, how wonderful to see you. You look a little tired, but then don't we all. Now sit and tell me everything that is going on." Martha led Jane to sit on a couch next to her. "Your phone call sounded very urgent. There must be something very important to bring you all this way on such short notice. But first, would you like something to drink?"

"Oh my God, you aren't going to believe this craziness. I don't know what to do. No, nothing to drink, thanks. Nothing like this has ever happened to me before. Thank you for seeing me on such short notice," Jane blurted out. She then took a deep breath. Jane proceeded to tell Martha of what seemed a miraculous healing of Johnny Oldshoes and the ensuing rumors and happenings in the neighborhood afterward. "I've locked myself in my room for a week hoping it would all die down but there is a daily stream of people to the center asking for me, begging me to come back and heal or help a child, sister, father, whoever. This is not what we are supposed to do! We are there to help people help themselves, get on their feet and take care of their families. And as you well know, I am no damn saint!"

"Oh my, that is quite a tale," Martha said with a half-hidden grin, "But remember my dear Sister, we are here to do the Lord's work, whatever that is, with love and compassion. Well, now that I've heard myself say that, I'm not sure what to make of this. It's not something I would have expected to hear from you. What do you want from me?" Martha looked up at Jane with the earnest face that she knew her friend wanted.

"You're the Superior. I owe you obedience. Tell me what to do. Order me somewhere."

"Oh really? Well if I order you to go to Rome and be the servant to a fat old Cardinal, would you march off and do it?" Martha asked with raised eyebrows.

"Yuck. Hell no! Don't be ridiculous," Jane answered with a grimace.

"All right then. I'm not in the business of just making things go away. Besides, you were never one to be ordered around. We'll come to a decision together, letting the Holy Spirit guide us. But first, it's been a long day for you and for me, so let's sleep on it. We'll meet after Mass in the morning and see what comes up." Martha got off the couch and reached down to hug Jane a Good Night. "There's a room down the hall way for you. See you tomorrow. God bless."

"Promise me this: don't leave me alone with this thing. I can't do this alone. I need your help," Jane pleaded, grabbing both of Martha's hands.

"I understand. I promise. Now rest yourself, get a good night's sleep, if you can. I'll clear my calendar to make sure we have plenty of time to pray, talk and decide. You are in God's good care. He won't let you down. I won't either. Sleep well."

Oddly, Sister Jane did sleep well, partly from exhaustion and partly because she felt safe in the convent with Sister Martha. The same could not be said for the Sister Superior, who tossed and turned all night, even dreaming of healing cripple children herself. This miraculous healing business seemed very strange, something out of a bad movie.

After 6 a.m. Mass the next morning, Sister Martha motioned for Jane to stay with her in the chapel. When they were alone, Sister Martha quietly said to Jane, "I know this seems medieval, but I am struck that we need some intense guidance. Let us prostrate ourselves before the Blessed Sacrament and pray for open hearts and a willingness to listen." Jane thought about giving Martha a skeptical look, but instead knelt down and lay flat on the carpet before the tabernacle. Martha joined her. They lay in silence for nearly twenty minutes.

Martha finally prayed: "Oh Lord, we are humble and sinful women who have strong ideas and forceful wills. We come to you upset, bewildered and confused. Calm our fears. Settle our minds. Help us detach from our needy and self-righteous egos, so that we can listen clearly to you. Guide us to do right, never spurning your gifts and grace, relishing your love for us and remaining grateful for your mercy."

Rising, she grabbed Jane's arm and whispered, "Come

on Jane, let's get a cup of tea."

With their steaming tea mugs, they walked to Sister Martha's room and again sat on the couch facing each other.

"Jane, several questions keep rattling in my head. First, what do you believe about this so-called miracle? You were there. Was it really a miraculous healing?" Martha asked.

Jane sat back and closed her eyes. "I felt a sensation when I was praying over Johnny. I don't know, a sort of tingling in my hand. He seemed very dead. Then he was suddenly alive and talking. He looked me right in the eye and said he had a message for me. He said that God wanted me to heal with love. Well, that could mean a lot of things. I mean, I hope I have been doing some of that all these years anyway, so it's nothing new. That's what we all try to do. It doesn't mean I have any special powers. I can't do magic, which is what people sorta want. Touch someone and they are instantly cured of cancer or palsy or something. But now the whole Mission District thinks I can do that stuff," Jane said throwing her hands up in the air. "It's crazy!"

"OK, Jane calm down. We know from crazy and you aren't, so let's try to figure out what God really wants from you right now. We never know for sure what God is doing with us. Sometimes we do something completely simple and innocuous, but people tell us later it had a big impact on them, maybe changed their lives. We don't know. But it's not us. It's Him working through us, using us. He wants to use you. Will you let Him?"

"Oh Martha, do you have to put it that way? Of course, that's what my whole vocation is about," Jane answered with a sigh of resignation.

"Jane, remember all the scripture accounts of Jesus' healing. What does he say? "Your faith has healed you." He never says, "Look at me, I got the power!" He always points to the Father and to each person's faith. That is what you must do. I know you know this, but you just have to get comfortable at pointing to the source, the real source of power."

There was a long moment of silence. "There is something else Sister." Martha waited patiently. "After Johnny Oldshoes came back, I did have a rush of feeling, very powerful, very special. I relished the thought of being suddenly very, very holy, you know God's most favorite. Somehow at that moment I was perfect, and you know what a perfectionist I can be. That's why I'm so afraid of this thing. It feeds my ego. Secretly there is a part of me that wants everyone fawning over me," Jane said in soft voice shaking her head.

"Of course, there is. Everyone's got one of those things you know. An ego. Don't run from it. Give it to the Lord. He'll handle it. You may not like the results sometimes, but somehow we always get humbled in the end. I've been thinking about this situation and here's what I think. I think old Johnny was there for a reason. And whatever felled him and your prayers that seemed to revive him was for a reason too. I think you should go back and deal with this head on. Perhaps a daily healing service where everyone can bring their sick or wounded and have a prayer over them. Create a liturgy. Read a gospel story of healing. Say some of the prayers from the missal around healing the sick, enlist some people to be helpers to assist you and do something that institutionalizes the whole healing idea for people. If it is God's will and people are helped, then it will continue. If it doesn't, it will peter out and you can stop," Martha said. Her enthusiasm was growing.

"Really? I think you're crazy."

"You know Sister Gertrude? She needs to get out of the cold weather here. I'll send her out to sunny San Francisco to help for you for six months. She's very prayerful and will be a rock for you. I think this is the right thing to do. You will have my complete official backing. And don't worry about your ego, you are doing this under obedience and at my direction, so stop fretting." Sister Martha stood up. "I'll have the whole community pray for the success of your new ministry. Come, let's have some breakfast. We have to get you a plane back to California."

The day following her return, Sister Jane put a small note on the front door of the recovery house stating that at 5:30 p.m. there would be a Vespers Service with Healing Prayers. Generally the yoga program was cleared out by 5p.m. and there would be plenty of time to set up chairs and candles for Vespers. She had no idea how many would show up, but hoped it was a small number.

At the appointed hour, there were just six. Four of them were familiar faces from the detox center. Betty Lou, a fifty-ish drug addict, semi-retired prostitute and mother of eight was sitting in the front row with a sweet smile on her face. She was gently petting her cat Chicha, a stray she had adopted nearly a year previous. She swore the cat was the reason she was able to stay clean for a year. The cat and a court order to attend an AA meeting every day for a year or go back to prison were beautiful incentives. Miles was a pale and thin, balding gay man in his late 20s. An extreme introvert with a bad stutter, Miles had taken a great liking to Sister Jane during his previous ten one-week stays at the detox center to get sober from cheap wine. Having spent most of his adult life in prison, Poppy, a black man in his late 60's had recently found religion and sobriety. He could work his favorite four scripture passages into any occasion or conversation. Bi-polar,

Maria, a middle age and handsome woman, had a willingness to take any pharmaceutical drug that was handy, regardless of shape, size or purpose. Two older women from the neighborhood, Mrs. Sanchez, whose elderly mother was going blind, and Ella, who always appeared sick from something, filled out the group. All sat in the circle of folding chairs.

Sister Jane started the service with an Our Father and three Hail Marys. She read a few prayers from the liturgy of anointing of the sick, followed by a gospel story of Jesus healing the blind man, and then she said, "My friends, we are here today to bring all our worries, our fears and our sufferings to God. To ask Him to heal us of all that ails us, that keep us from being whole and healthy and happy. Let us pray, Lord, we come to you humble, sinful and hurt. Look on us, with our small but real faith and heal us. Have mercy on our failings and through your power and love for us, restore our sagging spirits and give us health."

She stood up, walked in front of each person seated and lay her hands on each head, silently praying over them for several minutes. Then, she made the sign of the cross with her thumb on their forehead. All were silent. After she had completed the circle, she returned to her chair, sat for a moment with her eyes closed and then recited, "Glory be to the Father, to the Son and to the Holy Spirit, as it was in the beginning, is now and ever shall be, world without end. Amen."

When she opened her eyes, she looked at the six, all of who looked directly at Jane with full smiles. "Thank you for coming," she said and got up.

"Sister, I could feel da power of de Lord, yes I could. I feel so much better," Betty Lou spouted out, slapping her thigh.

"Yes, me too Sister. I feel, well, in fact I feel good!" Ella rejoined.

"Wonderful! Let's give thanks to God for this. Remember, it is He who heals and loves us," Jane said, as she tried to make a hasty exit out of the center to return to her room.

Miles stopped her. "S-s-s-s-sis-s-ster, you g-g-g-got da p-p-p-power," he paused for a moment, "Thank you."

"No Miles, you have the faith. Keep coming back." Jane took a few steps, then turned back. "Thank you Miles."

The next day there were five more people who came, and the numbers increased every day afterward, until by the second week there were nearly forty people in the room. In order to keep the Vespers service to a reasonable time, she spent less than a minute praying over each person. She decided to end the service singing the song "Healing Rivers", which gave her time at the end to get away quickly. There were no miraculous healings, no cancer cures nor limbs mended, but many people said they felt better and stronger and they could feel Jane's power praying over them. As it became a daily event and more normalized, Jane grew more comfortable as well and began to see it as just a part of her ministry at the detox center, like yoga, Twelve Step meetings, the painting and sewing classes, all of which were designed to help people live healthier lives.

Secretly, it became the favorite part of her day.

14

Father Cody placed a two-foot-high stack of personnel folders on Archbishop Peterson's desk. "These are the files of priests in the Archdiocese where there have been some mention of homosexuality, either in a letter sent in from a parishioner or some previous investigation due to a controversial sermon or public statement," he said, looking down on the mound of files.

"Good God. How many files are there?!"

"Over 155, Your Excellency. I might add that none of these priests were found to be in need of any disciplinary action by the previous administration. None of these priest were involved in any sexual abuse cases. Those files are separate and kept by our lawyers."

"Well, I will be the judge of that. Clear my calendar for the afternoon. This will take some time. Leave me to it," the Archbishop waved his hand dismissing Father Cody.

As the Archbishop began going through the files, he knew nearly none of the priests whose files had been placed before him. Most files contained accusations in the form of letters from angry parishioners who had objected to a priest's tolerant views in a sermon or who had spotted the priest marching in a Gay Pride parade, often leading their gay parishioners. Some accusers had seen the priest in a restaurant with another man who appeared to be gay. Many of the letters sounded like they were written by third graders tattling to a teacher about misconduct on the playground. There was nothing specific or anything that might be a violation of canon law but rather innuendo of association and moral outrage at the idea that the priest might be gay. Several letters stated they were carbon copying the Pope as well. The Archbishop wondered how many letters the Vatican received like the ones he was reading and chuckled when he thought how quickly they would be filed in the wastebasket. The Curia was notoriously backward when it came to administration, only installing voicemail on their phone system the year before and still not using email. Vatican bureaucrats like to keep everything the way it was, five hundred years ago. Even many bishops found that urgent and important letters to the Vatican didn't get answered for a year or more and the reply was usually typed on an aging manual typewriter.

As he moved laboriously through the files he was surprised to see one name he knew, Monsignor Al Pevehaus. As he looked through the file, there was a handwritten note, unsigned but on the Archdiocesan stationery. "Rumors abound that A.P. was involved romantically with a Mexican immigrant, recently deported. This indiscretion appears to have had a negative influence on a recent vote at the planning commission to reject plans for a new cathedral. A.P. has been transferred to the Holy See and is in their jurisdiction. No further inquiry is possible." He wondered whose handwriting was on the note, and why it was unsigned and undated. Surprised to find this information, he decided to investigate further but was unsure who to ask. He didn't want to involve his predecessor, the retired Archbishop O'Brien, who had moved to Southern California and was rumored to be a bit senile.

"Father Cody, could you please come in for a minute," he phoned to his secretary. As the priest stood over his shoulder, "Do you recognize this handwriting by any chance?"

"Yes, Archbishop. That is Archbishop O'Brien's writing."

"I see, thank you. That is all."

As he thought about this information, the Archbishop was conflicted. He liked and admired Al Pevehaus, not just because of his previous accomplishments and charming manner and his connections to the power structure in San Francisco, but also because of his easy "romanitas" way of understanding and discussing the Church and his obvious connections with Vatican insiders. He'd heard he was a favorite of several very powerful Cardinals on the Curia. He had wanted Al to be his ally and perhaps a confidant. Yet his predecessor had found something not quite right about the Monsignor and had worried enough to place a private note in his file. He looked through the rest of the folder and could find nothing else to incriminate or implicate Pevehaus in anything gay. Perhaps it was only a baseless rumor.

Five hours later, after going through all 155 files, the Archbishop had made a list of priests that were sufficiently suspect that they should be investigated further or given warnings. Most were on the list because they had marched in Gay Pride parades or had written notes in their parish bulletins expressing tolerance for gays, gay unions or homosexuality in general, though several were accused of having a homosexual relationship with another man. They would be placed on a watch list and officially notified that the Archbishop would tolerate no behavior that did not, by written, spoken or personal behavior, completely support the Church's teaching that all homosexual acts were sinful, evil and to be avoided under penalty of committing a mortal sin, and that all parishioners should be taught that a homosexual inclination was "intrinsically disordered" and against the natural law of God and all creation. Homosexuals could remain in the good graces of God and Church if they remained totally chaste and celibate, showing no physical affection to those of their same sex. Further, no person with a homosexual inclination, even though chaste, shall be encouraged to enter a seminary or otherwise apply for any church position normally open to lay people, such as a reader, Eucharistic minister or server at Mass. This was the teaching of the Church and Archbishop Peterson felt he had a personal commission to vigorously pursue his diocese's compliance with this teaching, regardless of the fact that this was San Francisco, the supposed "gay capital" of the country. He would bravely fight for the truth and right, regardless of how much he might be personally attacked, as had happened so recently in the park. He reflected that it was his role, his divine mission to combat the forces of evil that were infecting American society, even though it was unpopular and society seemed to be moving the other way. It would be his own private martyrdom. He was a true and faithful son of the Church and felt confident his reward would be in heaven.

Two days later, Father Cody brought another file to the Archbishop. "Your Excellency, I think you may find this situation is also of interest to you. It concerns a nun, one that it appears has been less than discrete about being a lesbian," Father Cody said with a slight smirk on his face. "It also appears that she may be acting as a priest in some manner."

"What! Who is this woman?" the Archbishop grabbed the file from the priest's hand. He read through the pages quickly. "I don't see anything here. What are you talking about?"

"Well, my sources tell me that she is holding daily healing services at a treatment center in the Mission. Some people think she has special powers and actually brought a man back to life. There haven't been any miracles lately, but she is quite well known and respected in the Latino community," Father Cody replied.

"What makes you think this Sister Jane Matthews is acting as a priest?"

"I understand she has anointed several people, clearly a sacrament act."

"Hmmm. And why is she known as a lesbian?"

"It just seems to be common knowledge. Apparently when asked, she does not deny it."

"What parish is this treatment center in?"

"Mission Dolores."

"I see. I wonder if our Father Fernandez knows of her. Call him and set up an appointment for him to come in. It's been a while since we've spoken. I'd like to ask him what is going on in his neighborhood and how our little project is coming along. He may have heard of this outrage." The very thought of young Father Fernandez, such a masculine and holy young priest, was a reassurance of the future of the Church and the kind of Latino man he hoped to attract to the seminary. He had high hopes for him and had thought of possible promotions that would give him great visibility in the

Archdiocese, particularly after the survey and the launch of a new program to serve the Latino population in the Mission.

The Archbishop put Sister Jane's file on his desk for further study. It was a scandal for a person to be openly gay in religious life, but to have a woman impersonate a priest was a crime of grave consequences. Several priests and nuns had been defrocked and excommunicated in the last few years for advocating or participating in the ordination of women. Pope John Paul II had expressly forbidden the topic to be discussed, much less acted upon and Pope Benedict XVI had enforced the ruling with vigor.

The last person Billy wanted to see in his currently confused state was Archbishop Peterson, but Father Cody had stressed that the appointment should be at Billy's earliest convenience and was important. He would not reveal the reason for the meeting. Pressed hard, Billy had agreed to meet the Archbishop the following afternoon. He dreaded a meeting alone but decided getting it over with as quickly as possible was the best strategy.

"Good afternoon, Father. Welcome. Please come in and sit here," the Archbishop held out his hand in greeting, gently lifting it for the expected kiss of his ring. Billy was guided to the couch across the room with the Archbishop taking a seat opposite in a chair. "Thank you, Father Cody," he said and dismissed his secretary.

Billy sat down and waited for the Archbishop to reveal what was on his mind. "So how is your mother doing Father?"

Surprised that the Archbishop even knew his mother lived in San Francisco, he replied evasively: "Very well. Thank you for asking Your Excellency."

"Good. My mother is still alive, you know, she's nearly 92. She lives with her younger sister in Los Angeles. It such a gift to still have a loving mother here with us."

"Yes," Billy replied, not knowing what to say.

"And the survey. How is that coming? I understand you and Monsignor Pevehaus have raised some money and are proceeding with the final design. When do you expect to begin sampling?"

"I would expect within the month. We have reviewed an initial draft and made some recommendations for changes."

"Excellent. This project is still an important priority for me and I look forward to what suggestions come out of it for new programs for the Church." The Archbishop shifted in his chair and looked more intently at Billy. "Father, I have another subject I would like to speak with you about, a some-what grave one, and I would like your complete discretion and confidentiality. May I have that assurance?"

"Yes, of course Your Excellency," Billy replied, trying not to show his nervousness.

"Do you know of a treatment center in your parish called..." The Archbishop could not remember the name. He stood up and went to his desk to retrieve the file on Sister Jane. "Ah yes, here it is, The New Hope Recovery House?"

"Yes. Your Excellency. I have heard of it. It's down near Valencia Street."

"Do you know the person who runs the center, a Sister Jane Matthews? I believe she is a Sister of Social Service," the Archbishop asked with raised eyebrows.

"Yes, I have met her. I think she has a very good reputa-tion in the neighborhood for helping many of the down and out, particularly drug addicts and alcoholics," Billy replied with a smile, curious why the Archbishop was interested.

"Well, I have heard some very disturbing reports, and here is where I must rely on your complete discretion." The Archbishop leaned forward, "I hear she has been holding various types of healing services, using certain prayers and anointing people in a manner that is strictly reserved for ordained priests."

Billy sat back, careful not to say a word.

"In addition, I understand that she is openly gay. Do you know of any of this?"

"Your Excellency, this is not what I have heard at all. I think she holds an afternoon Vespers prayer service where there are some prayers for healing, but there is nothing like the anointing of the sick. And I have never heard her say anything public about being gay," Billy replied hoping that he was diffusing the issue.

"Have you attended any of these services?"

"No, Your Excellency, but I have heard of them. They seem to give great comfort to people."

"I see. Well, Father, since this center is in your parish, perhaps you should attend one of these services. I would like a full report. Would you do that for me?"

"Of course, Your Excellency."

"Good. Well, the sooner the better. May I hear from you in a day or so?"

"Yes, of course." Billy started to get up to leave. "Is that all?"

"Yes, Father. But it has been nice seeing you again. I have great confidence in you. I could have asked any number of priests to investigate this but I choose you because I think you have promise as a priest and represent such a bright future for the Church. I'm sure you won't disappoint me."

15

Billy tried to make his way
through the crowd that blocked the door to the New Hope
Recovery House but it was difficult as everyone was so focused on trying to hear Sister Jane conduct the service. However once people saw Billy's clerical collar, they receded in
deference. There were nearly fifty people crammed into the
meeting room yet there was complete silence as Jane intoned
the familiar prayers of healing and forgiveness from Psalm 41,
"Happy are those who are concerned for the poor. The Lord
will help them when they are in trouble. The Lord will help
them when they are sick and will restore them to health."

Billy knelt patiently with the others as Jane moved
through the room, gently laying her hands on each head,
bending down to say a prayer into the ear of each person.
When she came to Billy, she smiled warmly, laid her hands on
his head and said, "May the Lord heal your vexations, may

He calm your troubled mind as you place your trust in Him. May he open your heart to love, His great love for you and those to whom He has chosen to love you so that you may live a joyful life, full of wonder and gratitude for His many gifts to you." Billy felt a calm settle over him, remarkable since he was so anxious just a few moments before, as he thought about the bind in which the Archbishop had placed him. "Trust," he thought, "That is what I have forgotten. Trust in the Lord. Trust it will all work out in the end."

With the large crowd, it took an hour and a half for the twenty-minute Vespers service to finish.

Billy saw Jane make a hasty exit and followed her quickly to tap her on the shoulder. "I need to talk with you. Now," he said with a look of consternation.

She motioned for him to follow her upstairs to her room. They did not speak.

As she opened the door, she flipped the light switch, marched across the room and threw herself into a large easy chair and sank down with her eyes closed. "I need a few moments to recover. Relax and have a seat," she said in a mumble.

Billy sat, closed his eyes and thought about what he was going to say.

After nearly ten minutes, Jane quietly spoke: "Hello Billy, how are you?"

"I'm a mess but not for the reasons you might imagine. I'm a mess about that too, but I have some terrible news to tell you and I don't know quite where to begin," he spoke evenly and calmly.

"Then get to the nub of it and we'll go from there."

"Well, I've been sent by the Archbishop to spy on you," he said matter-of-factly.

"Hah! Really? You, of all people. Why?" she said with a half laugh.

"He has heard about the healing services and he thinks you are trying to act like a priest, maybe setting yourself up as some kind of a priestly replacement or something. I don't know, I think he's crazy myself."

"What does he want you to do?"

"I am supposed to attend a service and report back to him what goes on. Let him know if there are any irregularities of canon law," Billy replied.

"Okay, so you were present today. Are there any?"

"None that I could see, just a lot of quiet prayer and healing. It was an amazing experience. I see why so many people come. I felt the Holy Spirit myself, a calming and soothing presence that certainly worked on me. I think you are doing a wonderful thing here. It is so needed and, as I can see, really appreciated by the people who come. But I have to tell you something else. The Archbishop has heard a rumor that you are openly gay, that you don't hide it."

"Oh, I see. He thinks I'm some loony dyke who pretends to be a priest so I can be a man. He is one sick puppy, your Archbishop," Jane said, looking out the window.

"Yes, I'm afraid so. What should I do? What should I say?" Billy asked.

"I don't know. He's not likely to let this go. You may tell him everything is fine, and he may leave it for a while, but I have a bad feeling. The hierarchy is so paranoid about women priests these days. They just get fanatical. The only people who have been excommunicated from the Church in the last twenty-five years are a couple of nuns and a priest who openly advocated for ordaining women priests. Not one bishop has gotten his hand slapped for covering up priestly predators, but say out loud that women should be priests and you get the severest penalty possible. It just seems to make them crazy."

"I know. My anxiety level is now back to pre-Vespers levels," Billy said with a half laugh.

"All right. Here is what I think. It's a radical idea, it's so far out," she said sitting up and looking directly at Billy. "Just tell him the truth."

"What do you mean?"

"Tell him what the service was like. And if he asks about the gay thing, tell him that as far as you know, I am faithful to my vows and that there is no scandal, but that I don't hide that I'm gay. That's the truth. Let's see what he does with it. I'm not going to play his game. I don't report to him. If he wants to do something to me he has to go to my Superior. Only she has authority over me. In fact I am doing these services under direct orders from her. And the recovery house is not owned by the Archdiocese, it's a private non-profit foundation. I don't think he can do much except make a lot of noise," Jane said with a relief, leaning back in her soft leather chair.

"Are you sure?"

"Yes. Now tell me what's going on in your world? How is love?" she asked with a big grin.

Billy sat back and let out a long sigh. "After I last saw you, I went to the beach to pray. I thought I received a message, a Divine message. I should immediately end the relationship with John, tell him I must be faithful to my vows as a priest and that we must never again be intimate. So I went to his house to tell him and end it. My resolve lasted about thirty seconds and then we fell into each other's arms, sobbing, telling each other how much we loved each other. So much for resolution and discipline. I just crumbled. We kissed and I was immediately back in Hawai'i and so in love with him. It felt so wonderful, so right. I know it's so wrong, but I can't help myself. Like I said, I'm a mess. I'm deliriously happy and terrified, all at the same time. He doesn't know what to do either but feels the same about me as I do about him. We decided to go away somewhere next Thursday and try to talk about it rationally. That sounds good to me, but in the back of my mind I know what I want to do, and it ain't talkin'."

"At least you're honest about it. If you can't be truthful with yourself about your real feelings you will get into a lot more trouble than you are in." Jane spoke with a sympathetic smile.

"There is one more wrinkle. John told Monsignor Al Pevehaus."

"Oh. Do you think he will tell the Archbishop?"

"No, I doubt that. You see Al Pevehaus and I had an affair once. When I was in high school," Billy said sensing his face getting a little flush with embarrassment.

"Yes, that would pretty much assure his silence." Jane fought showing a smirk.

"But that doesn't mean he wouldn't cause me trouble some other way. I just don't entirely trust him."

"Did he hurt you?" she asked with a slight tone of anger.

"Yes, but I'm over it. It's a long story. I'll tell you some time."

"So. Billy, just be true to yourself. Pray, keep putting one foot in front of the other, and let God lead you. There is so much to learn, about love, about yourself, your vocation, your faith. This is a great moment in your life. Embrace it, even the pain of it. You aren't alone and I just know some great good will come out of it. You will probably have to make some tough choices, but you will know when that time is, and you will know what to do. I pray every day for you. You are on a holy path. Trust that this is all part of God's plan for you." Jane got up and reached out to Billy, giving him a warm hug.

"Oh Jane. Thank you. I am so blessed to have you in my life. I never have to hide from you, I can be myself like nowhere else."

"I am so grateful for you, too. Now, give me some rest and let me know after you meet with the Archbishop. I want to be prepared. I'm sure I will hear from him. And let me know how the trip with John goes."

They hugged one last time and Billy left feeling very tired himself.

16

When Billy returned to the rectory, there was a message from Al Pevehaus waiting for him. This was a phone call he did not want to make, yet it had occurred to him that Al might be helpful with the situation between him and the Archbishop. Al had nothing to say on the phone other than he wanted to meet with Billy as soon as they could. They agreed to meet the next day for lunch at a cafe out in the Richmond District, a location where it would be unlikely they would meet anyone they knew.

Billy arrived late and found Al sitting in a booth at the far end of the cafe.

"Hello Father Fernandez. Try the corned beef sandwich, it's the best in the city," he said looking up at Billy with a wry smile.

"Hello Al." He sat down and stared at Al with a deadpan look.

"How are things?" Al asked.

"What do you think?"

"Difficult, I'm sure. Has John told you he spoke with me?" Al asked, trying to seem sympathetic.

"Yes."

"Well, Billy, you may not believe me but I thought I would see you and offer to help since I imagine you don't really have anyone to talk with about this. Besides, John asked me to."

"Yes, I know. I have seen him since you have," Billy answered.

"Oh. Well, he seemed pretty upset when I spoke with him last. I think this has all taken him quite by surprise."

"He and I, both. But Al I don't think you need to get in the middle of this. In fact, I think it would only complicate matters more. John and I will be able to handle it. I'm sure you have a lot of mixed feelings about it yourself since you are such good friends with both Becca and John. Thanks for the offer though. I have another reason to meet with you."

"I do have a lot of mixed feelings, especially given our history. I'm worried though. I care about you all and I hate to think of any of you getting hurt," Al said, sounding truly sincere.

They ordered two corned beef sandwiches and turned back to their conversation.

"What I do want to talk with you about is an incredible bind I find myself in with the Archbishop. I hope I can trust you to keep this between us?" Billy began.

"I am no fan of his, believe me. Yes, you can trust me," Al replied, holding his hand up.

"I met him yesterday morning. He seems to be on some sort of witch hunt and has asked me to spy on a particular

160

person he is suspicious of."

Al jumped in immediately, "Me?"

"No. Relax. At least not yet," Billy said with a laugh.

"OK, then who?"

"Do you know Sister Jane Matthews?"

"Afraid not. Who is she?" Al replied setting back into his seat.

"She is a good friend of mine. She runs a recovery house in the Mission for alcoholics and drug addicts. She's a Sister of Social Service and does a lot of good work."

"Why would the AB go after her?"

"It's complicated. She has been holding a daily healing prayer service at the Mission and a few people have been talking about what tremendous healing powers she has. The AB thinks she might be saying sacramental prayers or acting like she's a priest," Billy explained.

"That's ridiculous. What does he care?"

"Well, he has also heard that she is openly gay and the combination has him riled up."

"Hmm. I've heard he hasn't been quite himself since he was attacked in Buena Vista Park. This news makes me a little nervous. Tell you what. I have a friend who works at the chancellery office. Let me ask around to see what I can find out and I'll get back to you."

"Thanks Al. Let me know what you find out."

"OK. But keep me somewhat informed about this deal with John and you too. I want to know if I need to offer a shoulder to cry on either to him or Becca. I don't know what magic you worked on him in Hawai'i, but he is very smitten and it has brought up a lot of issues I don't think he has ever dealt with before, which doesn't make it any easier."

"Yes, I know. I love him, too. And if there was any

magic being spun, it was by Kauai. I was completely bowled over and more surprised than he was. You did try to warn me about Hawai'i but I was unprepared for how beautiful and otherworldly it was. I can't wait to go back."

Paying the bill, they left each other with a handshake.

"I'll call you as soon as I know anything," Al said as they parted.

That evening Al made a phone call to his source within the chancellery office. He was not exactly a friend but rather a priest that owed Al several significant favors, ones that Al wouldn't call in on a trivial matter but only if it was important, and Al had heard enough from Billy to be more than a little curious about what was going on with the Archbishop.

"Hello Bob, Al Pevehaus."

"Ugh, Oh hello, Al. Fancy hearing from you. How are you?"

"I'm fine Bob, how about you?"

"Good, thanks."

"Listen Bob, I have a favor to ask you. I'm trying to find out about someone, a nun, who might help me with this new survey I am doing in the Mission."

"Uh-huh."

"Her name is Sister Jane Matthews."

"Uh-huh."

"Have you heard of her?"

"Uh-huh."

"Bob, it sounds like you know something you are not telling me. What's her story?"

"Oh nothing, Al. I don't know her myself but I did heard her name the other day."

"At the office?"

"Uh-huh."

"And?"

"Well, Al, you know I can't talk about official business."

"Sure, I know Bob, but you can tell me something. I wouldn't ask if it wasn't important to me. Why is she being talked about?"

"Oh, nothing really." There was a long pause in the conversation which Al did nothing to break. "Well, there is concern about what she is doing down there in the Mission. Holding healing services and the like. A certain someone is a little concerned she may be one of those radicals who think women ought to be priests, a subject that is *verboten* you know."

"Yes, I know. That sounds a little farfetched. Anything else? Come on Bob, you can tell me."

"Well, people say she is pretty out there, if you know what I mean by *out*."

"Hmm. Yes, I get your drift. I hear there might be some sort of witch-hunt going on. Is that so?"

"Oh my, witch-hunt, noooo. What do you mean?"

"You know what I mean. That's something that could be very embarrassing for a lot of people, don't you think?"

"Yes, it could."

"So what's going on Bob?"

"Well, there's been a lot of looking at files."

"I see. Like maybe my file?"

"Perhaps."

"Is there anything in it?"

"There does seem to be a handwritten note. Honestly Al, I don't know what it says. You know I don't have access to personnel files."

"Uh-huh. Then how do you know there is a handwritten note in my file?"

"He asked me if I recognized the handwriting. It was O'Brien's. That's all I know."

"I believe you, Bob. By the way, did your file get a look too?"

There was a silence. "No."

"I didn't think so. Well, thank you for the heads up, Bob. Forewarned is forearmed. You be sure to let me know if you hear anything else. You can count on my discretion always, you know that. "

"Good night, Al."

"Good night, Bob."

Al sat back in his chair, suddenly feeling a little threatened. He had been suspicious that the former Archbishop O'Brien had heard something about Al that made him want to keep Al in Rome and away from San Francisco a few years back, but he didn't know exactly how specific that knowledge was. It would be important to find that out sooner, rather than later, especially if this new Archbishop was intent on searching out gay folk in the Church. He would have to lean on Bob to get him a copy, which despite Bob's protests wouldn't be that hard. After all, he was the Archbishop's personal secretary. But even with that information, Al began to feel the need for a little insurance. There was something fishy about the Archbishop that Al sensed from their first meeting, some internal issue that made the man very tightly strung, something that made him a little more than your average homophobe, some deep fear that drove his obsession about gay people. There had to be a clue about that fear somewhere. It was surely very hidden, very private. It would take some thinking about where to look and how to find it.

Al, as usual when he was feeling a little anxious, thought of Jake and the great time they had the week before. He picked his phone up and sent a text. "Jake, you around? Feel like hanging out?"

Al waited. Texts were so efficient yet waiting for a reply could be maddening. After five minutes he gave up and put the phone down and turned on the TV. He was too restless to watch TV so he decided to look at a little internet porn. That always made the time go by.

Fifteen minutes later, the gentle ping on his new iPhone told him his wait was over. "Hi, been wondering when I would hear from you. Tonight? It's a little late."

Al looked at his watch. It was 10:30.

"Too late for you?"

"Not too late, just not home right now. Could meet at midnight if you want. How about tomorrow?"

Al didn't want to wait. He wanted Jake right now and was frustrated that Jake wasn't available immediately. He was supposed to say Mass at 8:30, which would make it a very short night if he met Jake at midnight.

"OK, how about lunch?"

"That works. Where?"

"Still like sushi? There's a small place at Noe and 17th."

"C U there. Noon."

"OK, don't be late."

"K. Don't be grumpy. j/k."

"Miss you," Al texted, surprising himself that he typed something so intimate.

"Aw. Sweet. XOXO."

Al leaned back in his chair. He did miss Jake, there was something more than just an exchange of funds going on for him and he liked it. He wondered if Jake felt the same way. He was certainly very different from the other hustlers he had been with. There was sweetness, a vulnerability and a humanity that he never felt from anyone else in the 'trade'. And Al craved an emotional connection now as he felt increasingly alone and vulnerable.

Jake was only five minutes late. Al was pleased with the improvement. He had gotten there early to get a booth in the back as Nippon Delight was a popular place in the Castro.

"Hiya."

"Hey, handsome. How are you? Sorry I'm a little late, Muni again," Jake smiled warmly and sat down.

"Take a look at the menu, this place gets crowded and we should order as soon as the waitress comes over."

"I'm easy. You order, I'll eat anything."

The waitress appeared, Al ordered and they made small talk about the weather and the two cute guys at the next table. The food arrived quickly and Jake began to wolf down one sushi roll after another, obviously hungry.

"So, we going back to my place after lunch?" Jake asked.

"Yes, I'd like that. How soon is your next appointment?" Al answered.

"Hmm. That sounds a little bitchy."

"Sorry, I didn't mean it to come out that way. I guess I was a little disappointed not to see you last night," Al said apologetically.

"OK. Apology accepted. But you know you can't control my life just because we've gotten together a couple of times. I do have to make a living. Besides, I was with a sick friend last night, not a client."

"You are right, I'm sorry. I'm just under a bit of stress and feeling a little vulnerable."

"I'm sorry. Perhaps I can make you feel a little more relaxed," Jake said with a wink.

"Yes, you can. I'm sure of it."

They finished their food. Al paid the bill and was waiting for change when an idea occurred to him.

"Say, Jake. I'm wondering if you might know someone who could help me. I'm looking for someone who might do a little investigative work, something I think they call 'hacking'. Would you know of anyone in your world of friends who might do that kind of work?" Al asked, raising his eyebrow.

"Hackers are a dime a dozen. What kind of hacking are you talking about?" Jake asked.

"Well, a guy who could hack into someone's email maybe, or get into their computer from a remote site and look at what web sites the person might be looking at. That kind of thing, not breaking into a bank or anything."

"I do know someone who is pretty good at that, but it's not a guy, it's a girl, a dyke really."

"I don't care about that, I just want someone who is good at their work and can be discrete and trusted. Naturally, I would pay for their efforts. What's her name?"

"Emily. Sweet huh? She's one tough cookie though," Jake said with a knowing smile. "You don't want to cross her."

"Actually, she sounds perfect," Al said, thinking of how he would position this little job to Emily as protecting a fellow lesbian against a bigoted authority figure.

They left the restaurant and drove to Jake's studio in the Tenderloin. As Al got out of his car, he remembered that he hadn't brought along any of his little "helper" pills. Well, maybe I'll play bottom this time he thought. He had grown to depend on Viagra to give him confidence, but since he hadn't had a drink, he thought everything would work out.

"Say Jake, do you mind changing into that cute Japanese robe you wore last time? I thought it was pretty sexy," Al said as he unbuttoned his shirt.

"Of course, darling," Jake said as he slipped into his closet. When he returned, Al was lying under the covers of his bed. Jake pranced across the room, swaying in a sexy little dance that gave glimpses of his privates. "OK, roll over, time for Daddy's massage."

"I will, but don't call me Daddy, I don't like that," Al said trying not to sound too harsh.

"Sorry. Well, just roll over and relax. I'm going to make you feel good."

Jake proceeded to pour a lightly-scented oil on Al's back and spread it over his shoulders and back as Al let out an audible groan.

"Ah, that feels so good," Al said with difficulty as his mouth was pressed again the pillow.

"Relax and enjoy," Jake replied.

Jake massaged the muscles of Al's back and shoulders for about ten minutes, then moved down to his glutes and legs. After a few minutes, he began to play gently with the area around the butthole.

Al moaned.

"Do you like that? Want a little more?"

"Uh-huh."

"I have a nice little toy you might like. Stay right there." Jake got off the bed and found a dildo in the bedstand, twisting the knob at the bottom until it started to vibrate. "Let me know if you don't like this, but it's one of my favorites."

Jake slowly worked the device, teasing Al's hole with various movements, pressing forward a little aggressively only to retreat just before Al might resist. Al began to moan with a pleasure.

Jake leaned down to whisper in Al's ear, "Seems you like my friend here. What do you want me to do?"

Al hesitated. He liked to be the aggressive one and had only been a bottom twice before in his life, which were not of the best sexual experiences. On the other hand, it felt good to let go and have Jake take charge and pleasure him. The internal battle lasted nearly a minute when Al suddenly rolled over and said: "I want to play with you. Give me that thing."

"Sure," Jake said with a smile, though he was secretly disappointed that Al wasn't going to let him continue to indulge the priest in a way that made Jake feel he was tenderly caring for Al. He handed Al the dildo, slipped his robe off and lay on the bed on his back. "Go for it."

Al sensed that something has been lost in the energy between them. He looked down at Jake, admiring his slim, white body. His reddened nipples stood erect. But then, after a moment, he laid down beside him.

"I'm sorry. I just want to cuddle with you for a moment."

"OK, come here," Jake said as he reached over to put his arm around his shoulder. They lay together in silence.

"What's the matter?" Jake asked.

"Oh, I don't know. It's hard for me to let go. I just always want to be in charge, but I'm tired of being in charge too." Al spoke in a near whisper. "Sometimes I just feel weary. I'm tired of fighting the world, of pretending to have to protect myself."

"Let's just lay here. We don't have to do anything. I'm fine with doing whatever you want," Jake replied in a quiet, soothing voice.

"Thanks." Al looked up at Jake and leaned forward to kiss him. "You may be my only friend in the world," Al said with a sad, self-pitying tone.

Jake smiled. He liked this priest, but he was actually appalled at what he was hearing. He was a rent boy and Al was his "john." This was a commercial relationship and Jake knew better than to think anything different. He had had several clients who spoke this way, fantasizing that he and they were somehow boyfriends or lovers. Often after such a conversation, he would never hear from them again.

Al suddenly jumped up, looked at Jake and blurted out: "I want to fuck you!"

"OK!" Jake reached over to the bed stand and found a bottle of lube and a condom. "Fuck me hard," Jake instructed.

Jake began to suck Al and very slowly he became erect. He opened the condom package with his teeth, put some lube on Al and rolled the condom down his shaft, massaging it to get it harder. Then Jake lay back and spread his legs, rubbing some lube on his ass. "Come fuck me."

With a determined look, Al crawled on top of Jake and tried to enter him. However, without his Viagra, his erection softened and he had difficulty pushing in. He spent another five minutes attempting to revive his hard-on and penetrate Jake, but failed every time.

"Shit." Al threw himself down on the bed next to Jake.

"Relax, don't worry." Jake was getting a little annoyed at Al's manic moves from passivity to aggression and now back again. This session did not bode to end well.

"I usually take a little Viagra but I forgot the damn pills today. Sorry."

"Don't apologize, I'm fine. Don't beat yourself up. It happens to lots of guys, all the time. Just relax," Jake said trying to diffuse the anxiety he felt from Al.

"Don't you have a little something that might help?" Al asked.

"I might." Jake got off the bed again and went into his bathroom and came back with a couple of pills and a glass of water. "Here, try this. It should give you a charge."

Al downed the pills without asking anything further.

"They work pretty fast, so get ready to blast off!" Jake said with a grin.

Al felt an immediate rush of blood to his face and head and an intense racing in his heart. A glow of good feeling overtook him and a sense that everything in the world was good and fine and going to be wonderful. He had a burst of self-confidence.

"My that is nice. Come here, sexy," Al said pulling Jake towards him. They rolled around the bed as Al began to laugh, almost giggling like a child. "Come on baby, fuck me like you were going to. I wanna play!"

Jake laughed. "Sure. Let's have some fun."

Jake proceeded to spend the next two hours having his way with Al who was now eagerly enjoying every move that Jake made, alternately moaning, laughing, taunting and teasing Jake to keep the action going.

Finally, Jake collapsed on the bed. "I'm done, I can't do any more. Time to rest."

"OK. Do you mind if I take a little nap, I'm tired too. But that was so much fun!" Al said, rolling on his side. "Wake me in an hour if I fall asleep."

Jake shook Al awake an hour and a half later. He was fully dressed. "Time to wake up sleepy head. I have to go out and it's almost six."

Al woke up and groggily threw his legs off the bed. "Oooff. Where am I?" He looked around, "Jake?"

"You're at my place. Take a minute, it will all come back to you. Here's a wash cloth to wipe your face. Get your bearings. Your clothes are on the other side of the bed," Jake said as he ran his hand through Al's hair. "That was quite a session."

Al got up, a bit unsteady, grabbed his clothes and went to the bathroom. Ten minutes later he came back to put his shoes on. "So what were in those pills you gave me. It didn't feel like Viagra," Al asked, trying not to sound worried.

"Oh, a little cousin of my friend Tina. You certainly seemed to enjoy her," Jake replied with a half grin.

"So what does that mean? Is Tina crack?" Al asked, feeling a little stupid for not knowing much about drug nicknames.

"No. It's a weaker, different version of Crystal." Jake reassured Al, "You should be fine."

"OK. Well, I'm feeling my old self now." He started to head toward the door. As he leaned toward Jake for a kiss, he got a slight look that suddenly reminded him they had a financial transaction to complete. "So how much do I owe you?"

"Well, that was four hours plus the pills, let's say eight hundred," Jake said casually.

Al looked in his wallet which was nearly empty then remembered he kept an emergency stash of ten one-hundred dollar bills behind his credit cards. He counted out eight and handed them to Jake.

"Thank you," Jake said taking the money, then gave Al a quick kiss on the lips. "Oh, and here's the name and phone number of that hacker Emily you asked about. I sent her a text telling her you might contact her. I just used your first name Alvin so she'd know it was you and OK to talk business."

"Oh yeah. Thanks. See you soon," Al said, giving Jake one last kiss goodbye.

17

John pulled up to the rectory at the Mission Dolores Basilica in a lapis blue Mercedes convertible, one of his four cars and the one usually driven by his youngest son, Rusty. He texted Billy that he was waiting outside. Almost instantly, Billy came out the front door sporting a shirt he had bought in Hawai'i. He slid into the car and they drove off without a word. After three blocks, John pulled over, reached over, gave Billy a quick kiss and pressed the button to lower the top of the convertible. "It's a beautiful day. We might as well enjoy it."

"Where are we going?" Billy asked.

"Down the coast, I have us a private bungalow at the Highlands Inn south of Carmel. Have you been there?" John replied beaming.

"No, but I've heard of Carmel."

"Well, it's another one of those incredibly beautiful

places, so off we go."

Quickly getting on to the freeway, they made their way south. The open air convertible was fun, but not easy for conversation against the noise of the wind. Billy wondered if that was on purpose, but decided to just enjoy the ride. They barely spoke over the next two hours. Once they got to the coast, the scenery became as breathtaking as promised. As they drove, the world of San Francisco society and the Roman Catholic Church receded from their memory. Billy imagined he was entering into another magical place of adventure, much like Hawai'i, where the rules were lax and the atmosphere was sensual and carefree.

As they arrived at the Highlands, a five star resort on the cliffs several miles above Big Sur, John jumped out of the car, checked in at the office and returned with the key to the bungalow. Driving through the complex of hotel rooms and separate bungalows, the convertible came to a dirt road that led to a lone, largish wood shingled hut on a point. They walked through the front door of the rustic cabin surrounded by giant redwood trees to view the front bay windows overlooking the endless expanse of the Pacific Ocean. John turned to Billy, "So what do you think?"

"Wow! Fabulous! What a view."

"It's beautiful, quiet and private. A great combination," John said grabbing Billy into his arms. "It's so great to be with you."

Billy couldn't resist and eagerly kissed John with a passion that had been building up over the long, silent drive. Coming up for breath, they looked at each other with anticipation of the next move. John broke the tension, "Are you hungry? I know a great place down the road."

"Starving!" Billy exclaimed though he was more than

willing to put off a meal to keep the sensual momentum building.

As they drove further south down Highway 1, Billy was pointing out one after another of the beautiful views of the cliffs and the ocean. The ruggedness of the coastline and the sparkling colors of the water were breathtaking. It was an unusually sunny day for the coast, without a trace of fog, which often dimmed the picturesque vistas. John smiled and watched Billy's boyish excitement over discovering one of the most treasured drives in America. Finally they pulled into a parking lot and walked up a long ramp of steps to a restaurant perched atop a cliff that looked down the coast nearly fifty miles.

"This place is pretty famous for its burgers and of course its views. It's called the Nepenthe, which is an ancient Greek word for something that chases away sorrow or depression. It literally means the drug of forgetfulness. Of course, the views are unforgettable," John said, placing his hand on Billy's shoulder as they walked.

They sat at a reserved table at the point away from the rest of crowd and ordered. They made small talk, looking up and down the coastline, commenting on this gnarled tree or that rock leaping out of the water. Each could feel the tension between them rising. Finally Billy touched John's hand and looked at him with a serious stare, "So John, what are we going to do?"

"Oh I don't know. Enjoy ourselves?" John said with a smile.

"Well yes, I am really enjoying this. But the purpose of this trip was to talk out what is going on between us and what we are going to do about it," Billy replied, trying to put a serious look on his face.

"I know. But I'm just loving being with you and showing you this magnificent place. It's as special to me as Hawai'i. Can't we talk seriously later?"

Their absurdly oversized hamburgers arrived.

"OK, but we have to talk a bit. After this killer burger," Billy said with a laugh.

They finished eating, neither one able to finish their meal, paid the check and decided to walk down a path that started in the parking lot and headed toward to the cliffs.

"All right Billy, I'll go first. The answer to the question of what we are going to do is that I have no fucking idea! This is so new to me. I know I want you. I love you and I can't wait to get naked with you again. I also love my wife and my kids. I love my life and I don't want to give it up. I have all these feelings and desires that are new and incredibly intense, but I also don't trust them. My brain is telling me I'm a crazy fool and taking a very big risk by ever seeing you again. But I wanted to. I just had to. Plus, I can't even think about whether I'm gay or not. That's just not a concept I can deal with. So I'm stuck between a rock and a hard place and things are bouncing around inside my head like a billiard ball. That's what going on with me." John stopped along the path and looked at Billy. "I don't think that was very helpful, I'm sorry."

"You sound like me. I'm in the same place. I want you so badly but I don't know that I want to leave the priesthood and I feel terrible that I'm betraying Becca and my vows. It's just wonderful to be with you and I love you too. My spiritual guide says I should follow love, that it will lead me to the right place that God is leading me. So here I am, but I'm so scared I want to run as fast as I can. All my resolve just melts away when I'm with you," Billy spoke looking down. He plucked dead leaves from the bushes, absently throwing them down in front of him.

"So there's no answer. Let's just enjoy the day. We'll decide tomorrow what's next. My head hurts, I don't want to think anymore."

"OK," said Billy. He leaned over and kissed John lightly. "Where to?"

"Well, let's walk to the point, drive a bit further south, then head back to the cabin," John suggested. They looked both ways up and down the path and with no one insight, embraced for a passionate kiss.

Arriving back to the Highlands Inn around 4:30, they went to their cabin, feeling a bit tired from all the driving and fresh air.

"How about a nap?" John suggested.

"Great idea," Billy said popping off his shoes and flopping onto the bed.

John took his shoes off and lay down beside him. They kissed and Billy laid his head on John's chest. He said, "This is just so beautiful. Thank you for bringing me."

Rubbing his hand through Billy's hair, he spoke softly, "I'm in bliss."

They lay together, listening to each other's breath slow bit by bit. Embraced, they drifted off into a dreamy sleep.

An hour later, Billy lifted his head. John opened one eye. "Ugh, John I'm sorry but I drooled all over the front of your shirt!"

He sat up and went for a towel. "Don't worry about it silly," John called after him, " I love that you were so sound asleep." Sitting up he unbuttoned his shirt and threw it into the corner. "We should maybe get ready for dinner. I'm going to take a shower."

"OK," Billy said not exactly knowing how to reply.

John grabbed his arm. "How about joining me and

washing my back?"

Billy replied with a large grin, "Sure!" He gave John a long kiss.

They stripped down and got into the luxurious shower that had a large window that faced out to the sea. John adjusted the water and Billy unwrapped the soap.

"I've never taken a shower with someone," Billy said sheepishly.

"Well I've never taken one with a man, at least in private. Come here."

They embraced while John grabbed the soap from Billy and started to lather it up in his hands. "Turn around."

With John standing behind, he washed Billy's lightly-haired chest and stomach, gently rubbing him, encircling his nipples with his forefinger, then reaching under his arms with both hands and whispered into his ear, "You've such a beautiful body, you are so gorgeous. I can't believe I get to do this."

"You make me feel so good. See?" Billy replied glancing down to his sizable erection.

"I hope you feel how turned on I am." John laughed and thrust himself against Billy's butt. John then moved his soapy hand down to Billy's swollen gland, stroking it slowing.

"Oh my God. I'm going to shoot for sure. Stop." Billy said with a small jerk away. "My turn."

He turned toward John and grabbed the soap, lathered it and started to wash John's chest and arms. With a large smiling grin, looking directly into John's eyes, he moved down to his stomach and then kneeling took his erection into his mouth in a quick move and began to suck him, grabbing his buttocks firmly with his soapy hands.

"Now I'm going to cum. Better stop."

Billy continued to suck him as both of them moaned louder until John suddenly, involuntarily jerked away, shooting semen down the front of Billy's face and chest. "Ahhhh-hhh," he cried, falling back against the wall of tile, he grabbed the shower door handle.

John looked down at Billy's smiling face. "You like that?" Billy asked feigning innocence.

With a large sigh, John said, "Yes, oh yes. I liked it. You are so good at that. My word!" John was trying to stand up straight and regain his balance.

"Well, I can't say it comes from practice. It's been a long time."

"Come here." John embraced Billy and went down on his knees to offer the same as had just been done to him. After a minute, Billy lifted him to his feet. "Do what you were doing before." He turned around and John began to masturbate him from behind. It didn't take long for Billy to climax as John pulled him close to himself, kissing his neck and ears.

They finished showering and toweled each other off.

"Thanks for the wash, but I think you forgot my back," John said jokingly.

"We took care of other things."

"Let's get dressed, I am very thirsty. It's time for a drink."

They spent the rest of the evening enjoying a gourmet meal and a vintage Napa Pinot Noir. They talked about their childhoods. Billy recounted his years in Rome and his adventures with Father Filiberto, a not so famous priest who ministered to the poor people who sort the garbage at the dump in Rome. Neither spoke of Al Pevehaus as if by non-verbal agreement. Billy did not mention his mafia connected uncle and cousin. Though Billy felt some shame around those familial connections, he had done nothing wrong and didn't think he had anything to feel guilty about. It was a past he wanted to put behind him and he didn't quite know how John would react to the facts of the matter.

After dinner they took a walk under a starlit sky, holding hands when they were away from the lights of the lodge. Conversation died down and they walked in silence for a few minutes. Then John blurted out: "Billy, I'm going to have to tell Becca about us. I just think I owe it to her to be honest. We haven't kept things from each other, and she has been honest with me about some difficult things in her life."

There was a sudden chill between them and Billy let go of John's hand. "I understand. How do you think she will react?"

"I don't know. I've never had to tell her anything quite so threatening to her before."

"When?"

"Probably, when I get back."

"What are you going to tell her?"

"That I am in love with you and I want to keep seeing you, and that I love her and the boys and don't want to lose them either."

"Do you think she will throw you out of the house?" Billy asked, stopping on the path.

"I don't think so. I hate to say, but our crowd has a lot of unconventional marriages. People make allowances as long as there isn't a public scandal. Becca will understand," John said with little emotion.

Billy continued walking but said nothing. He didn't want to think about what John had just said and what it would mean to him. He decided to think about it later. He just wanted to continue to experience the magic of the moment and the beauty of the place.

They got back to their bungalow and decided to get some sleep for an early morning rise. Crawling into bed naked, they kissed and snuggled, but did not make love again. John drifted off to sleep quickly.

Billy couldn't stop thinking of John's words about how he thought Becca would react to the news of their affair. Much separated him from John, age, education and certainly money. But he hadn't thought of the vast difference of the culture between the old rich and the Latino poor. What mattered most to the wealthy was status and prestige, and public scandal was the enemy of that. Personal integrity was much further down the list of importance. With wealth came an easy belief that one could have everything one wanted. He could see that John wanted Billy and the excitement of their affair, yet he also wanted to keep the prestige and status of his life and family in Pacific Heights. It dawned on Billy that John had decided he really didn't have to choose one or the other.

As much as he loved being with John and the life it afforded, he knew that he had to jettison his fantasy that anything would ever come of their relationship. As attractive as John's proposition looked to Billy in his own circumstance, he knew that he could never live that way. He didn't want to live a secret double life, one day the erstwhile priest, the next day the pampered lover boy. What mattered most to him was family and personal honesty. Reflecting on John's words, Billy gained some clarity as to what he wanted, and that helped to relax him, which led finally to sleep.

Even though he did not sleep well, Billy was the first up in the morning. He showered quickly and quietly and was dressed when he shook John gently to wake him.

"Hey it's a beautiful day, wake up."

"Oh, my, what time is it?"

"Almost seven. Let's have breakfast and find a place to hike," Billy said, sounding a bit exuberant.

"OK." John asked, reaching out, "How about a kiss?"

Billy leaned down and gave him a short kiss. "Let's go, I'm starving."

"OK, OK. I'll be ready in a minute."

At breakfast they decided to hike the Big Sur trail and have lunch at the Nepenthe again. Billy reminded John that he had to be in San Francisco to say the 5:30 p.m. Mass. They would have to head back after lunch. John was a little disappointed that they would not have another erotic adventure in the room, but he didn't say anything.

On the three-hour ride home after lunch, Billy and John were each lost in their own thoughts. John rehearsed how he would tell Becca about their relationship. Billy questioned over and over again what God might be telling him. Did he have a vocation to be a priest? Could he really maintain a celibate life? The complexities of his life as a priest seemed easier to deal with than the complications and convolutions of a gay relationship, particularly with an older married man.

John broke the silence as they exited the freeway in San Francisco. "You are pretty quiet. What are you thinking?" he asked Billy.

"Oh you know, just thinking about everything. Wondering what's going to happen when you tell Becca. How can I face her? What would she say to me? I'm wondering what I'm going to say at the 5:30 Mass. Am I going to see you again? Small stuff like that," Billy said with a slight smirk and a sideway glance.

"Well, I'll let you know about Becca, but I don't think you have to worry. And I want to see you again, so please,

please don't disappear on me. I had a great time, just being around you. I'm confused, true, and have to deal with some things. But you touch something in me so real, so wonderful, so life giving, I can't live without it now. Life will never be the same for me since I met you. Give me time and let me, I mean, let us grow more together."

They drove on in silence.

As John pulled up in front of the rectory, Billy put his hand on top of John's. "Thank you so much for a wonderful day off. It was magic, again. You are so wonderful." He glanced around to see if anyone was looking, then reached over and gave John a quick kiss on the mouth.

"Good bye. I'll be in touch. Love you."

Billy got out, grabbed his bag and looked at his watch. He had ten minutes to get to the Church, change into his vestments and start Mass. He sighed and ran up the steps of the Church.

18

John parked the car in the garage and noticed that Becca's car was out. He grabbed his overnight bag and headed toward the door, which opened as if by magic when he reached for the handle.

"Welcome home," Pinky said, as he grabbed for the bag.

"Hello Pinky. Thank you. What time will Becca be home, do you know?"

"I think dinner time. There is only the two of you tonight," Pinky replied looking at John with a blank stare. John could tell there was some message behind those eyes but couldn't place it.

"Fine. I'm going to shower and I will wait for her in the garden. Please tell her when she returns."

"Yes, of course."

As John sat trying to read the morning paper in the garden, he downed two scotches in quick succession but in nearly an hour had yet to make it past the front page.

"Hello, darling. How was your little get away?" Becca called from the doorway, her hand clutching her briefcase. She had just come from one of her charity committee meetings.

"Wonderful, thank you. Please come join me for a drink. I want to chat," John said attempting to sound casual.

"Love to. Give me five."

Becca returned with a glass of wine in her hand, bent over to give John a quick kiss and sat down opposite him.

"How are you my dear?" he asked.

"I'm good. I had a delightful dinner last night with Dotsey and Spanky. We tried a hot new place that just opened on Valencia Street. Fancy a four star restaurant in the Mission! My how things have changed! It was *tres elegant* and the food delicious. Spanky had to pull some major strings to get us in, but then she and Michael Brewer, the Chronicle food critic, are as thick as thieves. We were treated as royalty, of course." Becca took a sip of wine and looked back at John. "Where did you go?"

"I went to Carmel, stayed at the Highlands Inn," John replied then emptied his glass. Within a second, Pinky appeared with a replacement.

"Thank you, Pinky. That will be all." John spoke dismissively.

"I took young Father Fernandez. He had never seen Carmel or Big Sur. He was quite delighted," John continued, looking at Becca with a raised eyebrow.

"You two have become quite the friends," Becca said, not looking at John.

"We have. In fact, I want to talk with you about that." John hesitated and found himself at a loss for words. A minute passed, then two, with no sound. "I find myself very emotionally attached to him." He waited for Becca to say something but she remained quiet and did not look at him but rather stared out at the view of the bay. "I'm not sure how I feel really. Just very attached."

"Uh-huh. It appears to me you are in love with him," she said with a sideward glance.

"I don't know. I might be."

"I could see this coming in Hawai'i. Are you sleeping together?"

"Yes, sort of." He hesitated, "I mean, yes."

"So, what else do you have to tell me," Becca said, now looking directly at John.

"Nothing. I just had to tell you this. I love you more than anything Becca and don't want to keep secrets from you. I can't keep anything from you anyway, you know me too well. I don't want this to come between us," John said with a quick look at Becca, then he drank another gulp of his scotch.

"Well, thank you for telling me. I guessed. You've had this gay side for a long time. I know you haven't acted on it, so better you should explore it a bit with someone safe and trustworthy. How does he feel?"

"Oh, he's confused as hell and struggling with his feelings. He doesn't want to leave the priesthood. He worries he is betraying you. He likes and respects you a lot."

"Well John, you should be careful with him. He's young and I don't think he knows the ways of the world much. He could be easily hurt, so be very honest and gentle with him," Becca sighed. She put down her glass. "I don't need to tell you about discretion, now do I?"

"No, darling, you don't. And there is nothing to worry about us either."

"I know dear." She reached across and placed her hand on his cheek and gave him a tender kiss. "I know."

John's eyes got slightly watery. He looked down. "Thank you for understanding."

"I would worry if you didn't tell me. You were very supportive of me when I had that difficult time with Jimmy, the boy's tennis pro. These things all work out in the end."

John grabbed his glass. "Time for dinner?" It was clear John did not want to discuss it any further since he wasn't ready to think about the end of his affair with Billy. He wanted to relish the present and was already thinking about their next trip together. It was a relief that Becca now knew, and if she didn't approve, she certainly didn't condemn him either. In an odd way, it balanced the books between them.

The following day John was off for a day of golf with his usual Saturday partners. Becca stayed home to work in the garden, a place she found serene and relaxing. Their gardener Max did all the real work, Becca just loved to putter, perhaps move a plant or pick some flowers for the table. She had been at it for nearly forty-five minutes when Pinky quietly appeared with an iced tea.

"An iced tea Madam?"

"Why yes, thank you Pinky."

He pulled a small table over to where she was kneeling and placed the glass down. Becca noticed that he seemed nervous and agitated. Instead of silently disappearing, he stood next to the table and did not move. This behavior was so unusual Becca turned to look more closely at him.

"Is there something the matter Pinky?"

"Well, it's not my place Madam, but have you noticed that Master John has been acting a bit strange of late?" Pinky said with a nervous twitch of his lower lip.

"Strange? Why no, I haven't. Why do you say that?"

"He seems very preoccupied and distracted. I was just a little worried something might be wrong with him," Pinky replied with a hesitation.

Becca was surprised that Pinky would mention his observations of John's behavior as he had never done so in the past.

"Oh, don't worry. He's fine," Becca said, turning back to the garden. "He's just infatuated with young Father Fernandez." The comment slipped out so quickly and easily that she did not see the instant reaction of the listener, who blanched with a look of horror. After a moment and hearing no reply she turned back, but Pinky was nowhere to be seen. She returned to her gardening but had the thought that she shouldn't have been quite so candid with Pinky, but then he was so much a part of the household, and he seemed to always know everything anyway.

Pinky walked quickly to his room. He closed the door behind him without making a sound, then threw himself onto his bed, and buried his face into his pillow and screamed. He rocked like a child back and forth for several minutes, then he pulled himself together. He rolled over and sat up on his bed. "How could she let him do this," he muttered, "It will destroy this house."

Pinky's mind imagined a complete catastrophe for the Williams family and himself. A scandal would ensue that would surely isolate the family socially and a divorce would be financially devastating. The house would be sold and with it the need for a houseboy, all because a cute young Mexican priest had seduced the man Pinky had dedicated his life to, a man he had loved secretly and silently for many years. The thought of the two of them, a priest no less, intertwined, naked and making love, enflamed Pinky with an unfulfilled lust and envy that created a need for immediate and severe vengeance. And Becca, the one person Pinky counted on to take strong action against this romantic intrusion upon their tranquil life, seemed blasé and unworried about the calamity about to happen. Pinky could not understand why she was not as jealous as he or as petrified of where it was all leading. It came to him suddenly that he must take action and take it immediately. He must expose this seductive home wrecker. He must have him punished and moved somewhere far away.

19

Al waited several days before beginning to take action on his plan to find some 'insurance' against any moves the Archbishop might make. He wanted to have an exact proposal to make to Emily, Jake's hacker friend. He called her late in the evening. After identifying himself and the referral from Jake, they agreed to meet the next afternoon at Café Flore in the Castro, a spot Al thought he was unlikely to run into anyone he knew and a place Emily would feel safe meeting a stranger. As he entered the glass enclosed outside patio she was easy to spot, a short androgynous looking person sitting alone at a corner table, black boots laced up well past her ankles, a black hoodie that covered most of her head except for a shock of bright red hair jutting straight out and three golden nose rings. Al had guessed her look correctly and came appropriately dressed himself, wearing black jeans, black tee shirt and black leather coat.

"Emily?"

"Alvin?"

"Just Al. What would you like to drink? I'll grab something."

"Hmm. A double Kettle on the rocks, squeeze of lime."

"Okaaay. I'll do the same."

Al returned to the table with the drinks.

"Cheers," he said, lifting his glass.

"So, who the fuck are you? You look pretty old to be a friend of Jake's."

"Let's just say we know each other. If we are going to have a professional relationship, you and I, do I have a guarantee that you will keep my confidence?" Al asked.

"Listen, confidentiality is my business. Keeping some and breaking others. I probably have more to lose than you," she replied, taking a sip from her drink.

"OK. I'm a priest."

"No shit! A fucking Catholic priest?"

"Yes, the very same."

"I fucking hate Catholic priests and your whole fucking homophobic Church. What the hell do you want from me?"

"Well, I gather from that response that you were raised Catholic," Al replied with a smile.

"Raised is not the right word. Try tortured. It's more accurate," Emily replied with a snarl.

"I understand. I've heard plenty of horror stories. But I'm not one of the assholes. I'm gay myself and I'm on a mission of mercy to help one of your sisters from some unjust treatment. If you will give me a chance to explain you may be interested in helping me. I can make it worth your while financially as well."

194

"Have at it, Padre. I'll try to keep an open mind, but you gotta know that I hate your whole stinking religion which has harmed more people than it has ever helped," she said turning slightly sideways. She took a large gulp of her drink.

"OK, here it is. There's a nun in the Mission who works with drug addicts and alcoholics, does a lot of good work, helps them out as best as she can, and in fact has a reputation for being quite a healer. She's also an out lesbian, doesn't really hide it. The powers that be don't like this and they are trying to get rid of her and stop her from helping folks."

"So who are these "powers that be"? Can't be cops."

"It's the Archbishop of San Francisco."

"An old fucking white man as usual. No offense," she replied, nodding at Al with a smirk.

"So, here's the thing. I think this guy is a total closet case himself and he's going after anyone who's in the Church who breathes gay, kind of a way to keep his gayness from overtaking him. You get what I mean?" Al leaned closer to Emily.

"You mean like all those sicko Republican congressmen who are rabidly anti-gay but pick up guys in the toilets for a quick blow job. Yeah, I get it. So what do you want me to do about it? If I went near this guy I would probably spit on him."

"I wouldn't want you anywhere near him. Besides, you'd scare the shit out of him. No, I want you to do some magic with his computer so that I, I mean we, can see what he's looking at in his spare time, maybe read some of his emails, so I know what his plans are and get some evidence that I can use to persuade him to back off from this good sister down in the Mission."

"Uh-huh. That's dangerous stuff you know. Can get me

in a lot of trouble. It's pretty risky. And this is awfully good of you. You sure it's only about the good sister?" Emily asked suspiciously.

"I know it's risky and I'm willing to pay you well for the risk. And yes, I think this guy may be coming after me too, so I have some personal reasons to do this. But I'm on the legit about the nun. Check her out yourself, her name is Sister Jane Matthews and she runs the New Hope Recovery House off Valencia Street."

"I will. My little brother's in rehab and naturally my father would only pay for a Catholic one. But I hear it's pretty good and he's getting better. So if she's as good as you say, I may help. I'll let you know," Emily said finishing her drink and standing up.

"OK. You want my number?" Al asked.

"Oh, come on, I already have what I need to find you."

Al wanted to reach out to shake her hand but they were already tucked into her hoodie. As she walked away, she looked back, "Thanks for the drink."

The next day, Al received a text: "2 grand to start. Meet at Café Flore tomorrow morning about 10."

As he arrived, Emily was sitting at the same table wearing the exact same clothes as before. As he approached her, she looked up and started to laugh, "Jesus, I could spot you're a priest a mile away. I thought you might try to dress undercover a little." She was looking him up and down.

Al had worn a sport shirt and sweater, but he did have black slacks and black loafers on.

"I'm not worried about being seen with you, are you? What would you like?" Al replied, feeling slightly embarrassed.

"Just black coffee."

He returned with two cups of coffee. He reached into his pocket and handed Emily an envelope. "All right, there's two grand in the envelope. When can you get started?"

Emily grabbed the envelope and put it in her side pocket. "So where is this computer you want me to hack. What kind is it?"

"I don't know. He has a personal computer in his room at the rectory where he lives. I think I can get access to it if need be. He also has a computer on his desk at his office downtown," Al replied.

"If you've seen the one at home, tell me what color it is."

"It was black, I think."

"OK, that tells me enough, it's not a Mac. I figured as much," she said condescendingly. "All right, now what is your email address?"

"Private or official?"

"Official. I assume you can email this guy and he would answer an email from you. So you will get an email from me under the name CrazyBitch. Open it, then delete it. Turn your computer off, then back on and log in as you normally would. Email this Archbishop some message in the early evening that he would likely reply to right away, probably from his home computer rather than one in an office. Can you do that?"

"I think so. What else?"

"Nothing. I'll let you know if this works. Otherwise, we'll have to try something else." Emily finished up her coffee.

"When will I hear from you?" Al asked.

"Within a week."

Al did as he was told though it was difficult to think of a reason to email the Archbishop and have him reply immediately after office hours. He decided to use a health issue, telling the Archbishop he had a concern about a heart condition that his doctor had recently noticed. He was pleased to see he got a reply that night with a message of concern and support.

Al texted Emily: "Should be good to go."

Two days later, Emily replied and told him to meet the next day at the same spot, same time and advised him to wear something less obvious. He arrived to find her just as he had left her, wearing the identical clothes but the hair was now green.

"Coffee?"

"Yeah."

Returning, he sat down and raised his eyebrows as he gently blew over the top of his cup. "So?"

"This guy does a lot of emails. Mostly really boring shit. A couple were in a mix of Italian, English and Latin. These guys still talk in Latin? For Christ's sake, Latin?" She took a slow sip of coffee and shook her head.

"Anything about Sister Jane?" Al asked leaning forward.

"Only one. It was email to another nun but it had a letter attached that was the real message. It wasn't a big deal, he simply reported that he had heard disturbing reports of her activities and was concerned. Pretty tame if you ask me."

"Anything else of interest?"

"Oh yeah." Emily paused to take another sip of coffee.

Al looked at her, "Yes?"

"The guy likes chat rooms. He spends a couple hours every night online chatting up other guys. They are all gay chat rooms, Squirt and Silverdaddies mostly. He likes to talk dirty, you know quickly getting down to what guys like to do. Stuff like that. Seems to really get off on bondage stuff, being tied up, and oh, spanking is a big one. He visited this site called BoySpanking.com, spent two hours there watching video clips. That's all so far. Nothing with kids or anything like that, just the regular kind of stuff."

"Well regular for you maybe, but not for an Archbishop," Al replied with a chuckle.

"I wouldn't know. I think you guys are all pervs. What else do you want?"

"I don't know yet. Can you read all his emails, even the official ones he does at the office?"

"Sure, but there's a lot of them. It will take some time depending on how long you want this to go on. I've spent over five hours already. You've about used up your two grand," she said with a certain tough look on her face.

"OK, well can you save stuff and I'll get back to you about going through it. I'll pay you more. I need to think of what I want to do next."

"All right. But let me know soon, this is crimping my social time," Emily replied, standing to leave.

"I'll be back to you shortly."

20

"Father Fernandez, this is Father Cody, the Archbishop's secretary calling. He asked me to set an appointment for you to report back to him about your investigations in the goings on at the Mission recovery house. It's been over a week and we have not heard from you. Can you come in tomorrow afternoon, say at 3:30?"

Billy had hoped the issue of spying for the Archbishop would just fade away. He had been dreading this phone call. "Yes Father. I will be there at 3:30," he replied.

He debated calling Sister Jane and seeking out a meeting to plot strategy on what to say but she had been explicit at their last meeting. He was simply trying to tell the truth and let the chips fall where they may. The trip to Carmel had distracted him. He now had less than 24 hours to decide what to say and to pray that all the right words would come out. The greatest weight on his mind was his own recent transgressions with John and the confusion he had about their relationship. As he thought about the upcoming meeting, he felt the need to confess his sins. He had a thought of confession to the Archbishop, but confessing to him would be completely self-destructive. The impulse to confess was a sure sign he needed to see Sister Jane, the only person in San Francisco he could totally trust. He had to take communion to the patients at St. Luke's hospital and from there he would go to the healing service and see Jane afterwards.

Every time Billy went to the healing service at the New Hope Recovery House, the crowds were larger. He arrived a little late. There was no hope of actually getting inside, so instead he joined the crowd milling outside the door. Waiting his turn, he eventually moved toward the altar for a blessing. As Sister Jane laid hands on his head and prayed, he looked up and told her quietly he wanted to see her afterwards. She nodded.

It took nearly a half hour for the crowds to clear out after the service. He followed Jane back to her residence. Climbing the stairs to her room, he could see how tired and weary she was. The service seemed to have drained all the energy from her.

"The crowds are getting bigger Jane. You are touching a real need here," Billy said trying to cheer her but the look he got back was one of exhaustion with a faint smile.

"Yes, and its taking me longer and longer to recover afterwards. It's a wonderful experience but I'm not sure how long I can keep this up."

"Thank you for taking the time to see me."

Jane collapsed into a sofa chair in the corner. Billy pulled up another chair near her, "I'll try to keep it short, but I have two reasons to see you. The first is that I'm seeing the

Archbishop tomorrow to report on you. Anything you want me to say or not say?" Billy asked.

"No. I trust you. Be honest and tell it as you experienced it," she replied leaning her head on her hand.

"The second reason is that I need to confess to you, I need to clear my head and ask for your guidance."

Jane sat up straighter and suddenly was more invigorated.

"John and I went away a couple of days ago for little trip to Carmel. A sort of lover's getaway," Billy began.

"Yes? How was it?"

"In many ways, it was just as magical as Hawai'i. Carmel is a very beautiful place. It was fun to get out of town. And I was thrilled to be with him," he said with a pause and a deep sigh.

"Nice. Did you learn anything?"

"Yes, I guess so. I'm very conflicted. And I don't know what the hell I'm doing," he said pausing again to look out the window. "It's wonderful to be with him, and it's very nice living in such a rich way. I mean everything with John is first class, the best money can buy. I have never lived that way, and it's quite an experience. We go to the most beautiful places. Everything is so enchanting. It's like I'm transported to another planet, a totally different world."

"I don't hear any conflict. How does he treat you?" Jane asked.

"Oh, he's totally respectful and sweet. He loves showing me new things and he stares at me a lot, I mean, just looking at me with this glassy eyed adoring look. Part of me loves it, but sometimes it's a bit unnerving."

"Go on," Jane said after Billy paused.

"OK, we had sex and I feel guilty that I'm breaking

my vows, and he is too. I mean there's no way not to think of this as sinful, but it also feels so natural and loving too. And I like it," he paused again. "So I feel very conflicted about that. Plus, when we were on a walk, he said something that has been bothering me. He said he was going to tell his wife about us, and that she would understand, and it wouldn't really change anything with her. He said things like this "aren't that uncommon with their friends." What does that mean? How could that be?" he said leaning forward excitedly and looked at Jane with his eyes blazing. He fell back into his chair. "I guess I'm just another passing fancy."

"So Billy, what did you think this relationship would be?"

"I don't know. I guess I really didn't think about it. I'm just so confused. I guess I'm the mistress or something," he said shaking his head.

"Yes, you are. You need to decide if you want to play that role, and for how long."

"No, I've been there before. I remember what happened last time. I got deported. Thrown aside when it got inconvenient." Billy paused and looked out the window. "Thank you Jane, I think I'm a little clearer about this now. I'm a fool."

"Now wait, don't be so hard on yourself or John. What else are you learning from this affair of love?"

"That I'm easily swayed by money?" he said jerking his head back to the side.

"No. I don't think so. Come on. May I suggest that you have a lot of love inside you and you need to share it with someone, or many someones. You can't keep it bottled up. Find more ways to love people and let them love you. Secondly, you are a sexual man, and I guess you need to decide if celibacy is going to work for you, or against you. That will be a difficult decision and you need to take your time with it, maybe even experiment more with it. Sexual desire is God-given. It's what draws us out of ourselves. It's not sinful and I hope you don't think of it that way. You'll have it the rest of your life, so make peace with it. Priests are not eunuchs. In fact, if you were a eunuch, you know, even the Church wouldn't ordain you. So love that part of you and pay attention to it."

"I hear what you say, but I'm having a hard time with it right now. I think I'm pretty clear that this relationship isn't what I want, it's not going to work for me and I need to end it," Billy said firmly.

"That's your decision. Be grateful for it and be grateful for John. He sounds like a nice man and I'm sure he is as surprised by it all as you are. Be kind to him. By telling his wife, he certainly shows some integrity," Jane counseled with a tired smile.

"You are so good. Thanks for listening to me. You look beat, I think I should leave you," Billy said starting to stand up.

"Wait. Let's say a prayer," Jane said. She leaned forward and grabbed Billy's hands in hers. "Lord Jesus, we come to you with our burdens, our confusions, our conflicts, our hurt feelings and our need to be healed. Let your love come into our hearts, help us to believe you are guiding us, that everything that happens to us in our lives is your invitation to learn to love more and better, that everything has its purpose and we are grateful. Forgive us our failings so that we may learn to forgive other's theirs. Always keep us close to your love, Amen."

Billy looked up and bathed himself in Jane's warm smile. "Thank you Sister."

"God Bless, Billy," she said leaning back in her chair

looking ready for a short nap.

Billy waited twenty minutes in the reception area at the chancellery office for his appointment with the Archbishop. The longer he sat the more anxious he felt. Finally, when he was shown into the Archbishop's office, he was directed to sit in a chair facing the leader while Father Cody stood at his side.

"Now, Father, tell me what you have learned about this nun and her machinations. I keep hearing more and more about her," the Archbishop said curtly.

"Well Your Excellency, I have attended several of her healing sessions at the center. They are very popular. Every time I went, there were more people in attendance. They are really quite simple. It is a Vespers service with songs, psalms and a few prayers from the Office. There is usually a scripture reading, often around one of Jesus' healing stories. Then people kneel and Sister Jane goes around the room, lays her hands on each person's head and says a quiet prayer. A decade of the rosary is said at the end of the service and that's it." Billy spoke is a factual, low-key manner as best as he could.

"I see. Does she use oil? Does he anoint anyone?"

"Nothing like that that I've seen. Just simply praying," Billy replied.

"Um-huh. What about espousing herself as a Lesbian. Are there a lot of masculine women around?" the Archbishop asked raising his eyebrows.

"Nothing like that that I have seen."

"And that's everything Father, you are not leaving anything out?"

"No sir. I don't think so."

"I see, Father. Well, there is another matter. Yesterday,

I received this letter, handwritten and unsigned, but it disturbs me greatly. I will read it, 'Dear Archbishop, Did you know one of your priests is destroying a happy marriage of two wonderful Catholics? He has seduced the husband into a disgusting affair and will ruin many lives. His name is Father Fernandez. Please put a stop to this wicked behavior.'"

Billy sat stunned, looking at the Archbishop. He could not speak but felt his face turn a deep red.

"Well Father, what do you say to this? Is it true?"

Billy still could not speak.

"You must answer your Archbishop, Father Fernandez," Father Cody interjected.

"Yes," Billy whispered.

"I am deeply disappointed, Father, deeply disappointed. You must end this affair immediately. Whoever this man is, you must cease any contact with him. I'm afraid I must suspend you from your priestly duties and privileges. Father Cody will inform your pastor. I will take a few days and pray over this matter before I decide what your penance will be and what shall happen to you. This is a grave sin and could be a very real scandal for the Church. I suggest you commit yourself to prayer and repentance. You are dismissed." The Archbishop turned away and shuffled some papers. Father Cody opened the door for him to leave.

Billy stumbled out of the chancellery office in complete shock, ashamed and angry. Who could have written that letter? John? Becca? He doubted that. He didn't know what to do next, but the idea came to him that Al Pevehaus might help. He called him on his cell phone immediately upon reaching his car.

"Al?"

"Hello, Billy. Listen can I call you back, I'm kind of in the middle of something," Al replied, sounding distracted.

"OK, but I have to tell you I've just been suspended and the AB knows about John and me," Billy blurted out.

"What! Oh shit. Wait." Al muffled the receiver to speak with the person he was with. After a moment he came back on. "All right, I can talk for a short while now. Tell me what happened and don't leave out any of the details."

Billy recounted his report about Sister Jane to the Archbishop, then the surprise bombshell with an anonymous letter that exposed the relationship with John. "I am suspended until the Archbishop decides what penance I must do and what he will do with me."

"Was anyone else present at this meeting?" Al asked.

"Yes, Father Cody, the Archbishop's secretary."

"OK. So we have a couple of days to deal with this. I'll call John and tell him. You go back to the rectory and relax. I know this sounds really bad, but it isn't. This isn't the first time something like that has happened and in the end a little groveling and a few 'mea culpas' will sooth the AB and everyone will forget about it. As long as it's not about kids, there's no legal exposure. I'll call you later tonight," Al said in a most competent and authoritative voice.

"Thanks Al. I'm really sorry to drag you into it," Billy said apologetically. However he was relieved that Al sounded so upbeat and that he was willing to help.

21

John put his cell phone down on
the desk in the library. He stared out the window at the beautiful view of the bay before him but he could see nothing. A
rage overtook him that he had not felt since he was a child.
Only one person could have written that letter, but he just
couldn't get his mind around the idea that he would be betrayed by someone so close to him, so loyal, so much a part
of his daily life, a person he had grown to love over so many
years. His thoughts turned to revenge, even to violence. He
had to get control over himself. He walked down the hall to
the kitchen.

"Becca! Come with me," he almost shouted upon seeing his wife standing near the kitchen window. She looked
at him and seeing his anger pulled her head back, but dutifully followed him to the library. He almost slammed the door
closed.

"I have been betrayed!" he shouted.

"What are you talking about?"

"Pinky has written a letter to the Archbishop exposing my relationship with Father Billy, who has been suspended in disgrace," he said as his face turned a vein-popping purple.

"Oh my God, you are kidding. This can't be! Were we named?"

"No. But that doesn't make any difference. How dare he interfere with our lives? How dare he!"

"OK, now calm yourself, John. Sit down, let's talk about this. How did you find out?" she asked, calmly trying to diffuse some of John's anger.

"Al called and told me. Billy told him that the Archbishop had received an anonymous letter accusing him of breaking up a wonderful Catholic marriage. Billy must feel terrible. I feel awful that I have gotten him into such a mess. And to think that Pinky betrayed me. My own servant. I'm beside myself, I can't think of why he would do that."

"How do you know he wrote the letter?" Becca asked.

"Who else could it be? *You* certainly wouldn't do anything like that and no one else could possibly know. He's been acting strange lately. I could feel it. It had to be him. That little bastard!" John clenched his fist. "He's fired, that it. No severance, no recommendation. He'll never get another job in this city."

"All right, now let's think this through, John, before we take any action. We must be careful here. We don't want to create any scandal ourselves. You know how servants talk. Would you really fire him? Could you live without him? How would we explain it to the boys? And to our friends?" Becca looked at John inquisitively.

John sat back and thought for a minute. Pinky was an

essential part of his daily life as well as the whole family. He had dressed John nearly every day for twenty-five years. He provided a level of service that made everyday living so very comfortable. He ran the household with efficiency and honesty. He was the model of an upper class servant and friends were envious. Simply firing Pinky wouldn't be easy and it would raise a lot of questions that John didn't want to answer. Stonewalling questions from their friends would only lead to exaggerated rumors and innuendos that had to be avoided. His rage had not dissipated but he was becoming more conflicted. He felt trapped. He had to do something.

"John, perhaps it's best to confront Pinky with this information and see what he has to say for himself. But don't make any rash decisions. Hear his side of the story, if there is one, and then let us decide afterwards."

"Yes, OK. We are certainly in a spot. Why don't you go find him while I try to get my emotions under control." John stood up and walked to the window. "Maybe I'm jumping to conclusions."

Becca opened the door and immediately saw Pinky standing in the hall looking anxious. "Pinky, please join us," she said, casually. She turned and he followed her in.

"Pinky something has come up," Becca began, taking the lead. "Someone has written a letter to Archbishop Peterson accusing our friend Father Fernandez of some terrible things. Would you know anything about this letter?"

"Me? No! Why would I know about this?" Pinky replied nervously.

"Because it was about Father Fernandez and me, that's why!" John barked.

Pinky blanched.

"You are the only one who could have written that letter," John said, his anger rising.

Pinky replied desperately, "There was nothing about you."

"So it was you! Why would you do such a disloyal thing? Explain yourself," John shouted.

"Oh, Master!" Pinky cried out, falling to his knees in front of John. "Because I love you and the Madam and this wonderful family and I didn't want to see it destroyed." Pinky broke into tears, "I love you so much, I always have!" He was nearly sobbing, something neither John nor Becca had ever seen.

"Oh Pinky. This was wrong. You should have come to me," Becca said.

Pinky turned to her, "Oh, I could never have explained it to you. I just wanted to save our family," he said, then fell into a convulsion of crying.

John put his hands on his head and looked at Becca with exasperation. She tilted her head to him as if to encourage his understanding of Pinky's plight.

"All right, all right. Stop your crying. What you did was very stupid and has caused Father Fernandez a great deal of harm and I'm very angry about it. Whatever you thought, there is no threat to this family. You let your emotions get the better of you. Leave us for a few minutes. I just don't know what to do about this and I don't know if I can ever trust you again," John spoke with a reprimanding tone.

Pinky rose to his feet, wiped his cheeks, straightened his white coat and stood erect. "Yes Master," he replied, then turned and left the room as he normally would have done.

Once the door was shut behind him, Pinky smiled to himself with a look of satisfaction on a stellar performance.

"Oh, John, you can't fire him. Didn't you see how distraught he was? He only did it for us," Becca implored.

"Yes, yes. But still, he betrayed my confidence. He never said a word to me or you about his fears. He should have said something! Instead he took matters into his own hands. I'm not sure I can ever really trust him again." John was circling the couch. "But I don't see how we can fire him either. Besides how would we ever replace him? I mean our friends have a horrible time finding reliable help these days. Well, if Billy ever comes to this house again, he had better treat him with complete respect," John said with resignation.

"I'm sure he would. Pinky is the consummate professional. I'll talk with him, I think I could be more rational than you. It's a tragedy that young Father Fernandez got hurt in this little domestic affair." Becca got up to leave. "Oh and by the way, Patsy and Bim invited us to the yacht club for dinner Friday night. Can I confirm?"

"Sure," John shrugged.

22

Al plotted out his plan of attack
in the darkness of his rectory bedroom. He had retreated there
after the phone call from Billy. Though the foggy gray afternoon hid the sun, he pulled the blackout curtains closed
because he wanted total darkness to think more clearly. Obviously Billy was now in the Archbishop's spotlight, and by
association he might be as well. What he needed to find out
was if the connection between he and Billy during Billy's high
school years had been discovered. There was that secret note
in his file. That would determine how much real danger Al
was in. He would have to wait a few hours, until later in the
night, to call Bob Cody, the Archbishop's secretary, and try to
get some confirmation of how events were unfolding. He had
already dealt with his friend John. He doubted that Becca had
sent that letter and was immediately suspicious of Pinky. He
had alerted John to his fears. As he sat in the dark, he thought

of what move he could make against the Archbishop and what role Emily could play in helping him.

As he sat waiting until he could call Bob Cody, his anxiety level began to rise. Even though it was barely past four, he poured a large glass of scotch to calm his nerves.

A second glass triggered his thoughts of Jake. The boy had become a more and more important part of his life, a soother of fears, a connection for sex and a taste of intense emotional connection. Most of all, he was someone who made Al feel alive and valued. He had come to believe that Jake really cared for him, enjoyed his company and thought him special. He discounted that he paid Jake a handsome fee every time they saw each other, rationalizing the payment as a gift to help support someone who was a starving artist, someone just getting their life together, conveniently forgetting Jake made his living by hustling.

A third scotch led to loneliness and a mild case of self-pity. Jake was the solution, so he texted him. A quick response set their time for 10:30 p.m. The fast, positive answer helped Al feel good immediately.

At half past seven, he called Bob Cody.

"Hello Al, I thought I might be hearing from you. I really can't help you here. Your boy is in real trouble," Bob said, trying to sound sympathetic.

"I know Bob. Well, he made his own mess, now he has to lie in it. I called because I need to know if there is some link to me."

"Uh, no, not directly."

"Bob, I just get the feeling you are not being entirely honest with me. This is serious. Your man there means business and he sounds like he's got a real bee in his bonnet. Now tell me what he knows. You know I know you know, so stop the bullshit," Al said putting force into voice, working hard not to slur his words.

There was a long pause. "He knows you knew Billy Fernandez in high school and that he is probably the one mentioned in the note O'Brien put in your file. He's asked me to do a lot more research into both of you and that wacky nun in the Mission."

"OK, that's better. What's he going to do about it?" Al pressed.

"I honestly don't know. He's got this thing about rooting out gays in the Church, says they are agents of the devil, sapping the diocese of its moral strength. He's a little nuts about this issue. But I don't know what his plans are. He hasn't told me."

"Well, I guess he'd better not find out about you then Bob. Don't worry I'll keep your secret, just let me know if you hear what his next move is. Forewarned is forearmed. For both of us." Al said. He hung up the phone.

It was definitely time to spring into action. He roused himself from his lethargy and texted Emily: "Need a crash meeting, have some more work for you."

"Best is tomorrow at lunch time. Orphan Andy's," came the reply.

Al arrived at Jake's place twenty minutes early and waited in his car across the street. After a few minutes, a white-haired, overweight, professional-looking man emerged and looked both ways down the sidewalk. He then proceeded to his car a short distance away.

Al was instantly jealous and angry. He jumped out of his car and started toward the man, who drove away quickly not even seeing Al. Unnerved, he headed toward Jake's door in a rage. Pounding on the door, Jake finally opened it slightly, and Al burst in.

"Hey, what's up?" Jake exclaimed, backing away.

"Who was that guy? A trick, I suppose?" Al spit out.

"Excuse me? That's none of your business! It's my business, remember?" Jake shouted. "You have no right to come busting in here. If you can't calm down, then leave!" Jake was naked, drying himself with a towel.

Al threw himself on the bed face down. After collecting himself, he rolled over.

"Oh Jake, sweetie, I'm sorry. I've had a hard day and I've missed you," Al whined apologetically.

"And you're a little drunk too," Jake replied, drying his hair.

"Well, maybe a little, but that won't matter. Come here, you naked gorgeous man!"

Jake wrapped himself in his towel and walked toward Al. Al wrapped his arms around his waist and buried his nose in Jake's navel. "Be nice to me, I need you."

"I will if you stop acting like a jealous school girl. Now tell me what's got you so upset," Jake replied, combing his fingers through Al's thinning gray hair.

"Oh, it's a long story, but I think my Archbishop may be after me and a friend of mine. I need to stop him. It's got me a little unnerved that's all," Al replied, lying back on the bed. "I just feel so alone sometimes."

Jake softened his demeanor. "Well you've come to the right place. Here, let's get these pants off. And your shirt. You have too many clothes on to be comfortable." Jake got onto the bed and let his towel drop. Now both were naked. They kissed and Al moaned with resignation and relaxation.

"Roll over and I'll give you a little back massage," Jake suggested.

Al lay quietly for ten minutes. It appeared to Jake that he might have fallen asleep. Suddenly, Al turned his head upward, "Say, do you have any of those fun, little pills?"

23

Al awoke the next morning

around eleven, fully clothed in his bed. He felt groggy and
disoriented. He looked at the clock, remembering that he
couldn't fall asleep after he had gotten back from Jake's. It
was nine o'clock the last time he had looked; he had slept just
two hours. He felt shaky and wired. Slowly, the events of the
previous day returned to him. "Shit, I have to meet Emily in
an hour," he muttered aloud to himself. He got up off the bed
and stumbled toward the shower. "Oh God, I feel terrible."

He found some codeine pills he had saved for such an
occasion and took four. After the shower he felt better but
noticed his hands shaking strongly as he pulled on his pants
and buttoned his shirt.

As he entered Orphan Andy's, a coffee shop in the center of the Castro District, he saw Emily sitting in the last booth
sipping a coffee.

"Hi."

"You look like shit. Long night?" she blurted out.

"Yes, what I can remember of it," he replied trying to smile.

"Well, I don't have much time so let's get down to business."

The waiter appeared and Al ordered two 7-Ups. He was feeling very dehydrated. He had no appetite.

"All right. Our friend is definitely going on a rampage. I need some visual proof of some of his nighttime interests, something I can show to him that would suitably intimidate him into backing off. It's not just me. It's several people including that nun in the Mission he's after. I need it fast," Al said as he gulped down his first drink.

"Is that all?" Emily asked.

"Yes, why?"

"Well, I already have all that, I just haven't shown it to you. I've recorded him online for several nights and enabled his video camera so that I have him video chatting with guys, even jacking off to some porn clips," she said, casually sipping her coffee. She grinned, "Will that do?"

"Yes, I think so," Al replied beaming with a glee. "How much?"

"Oh, since it's for a good cause and I don't have to do any more work, how about 500?"

"You're sweet! I'm fresh out of cash but there is an ATM around the corner. I'll pay you now. How will I get delivery?"

"It'll be in your inbox when you get home. Let me know if everything comes through all right. You should make some back-up copies and store them on memory sticks, just in case." Emily finished her coffee and then got up. "Let's go, I have class in an hour."

Al printed out the letter and read it over again:

"Your Excellency:
Please review the files on the enclosed memory
stick in complete privacy.
The pictures and videos that you see can and
will be widely distributed on the internet and the local
press if you fail to follow these instructions:
1. You are to restore Father Fernandez to his
full faculties and cease any actions against him.
2. You are to drop any inquiry into the actions
of Sister Jane Williams and the New Hope Recovery
House.
3. You are to drop all further inquiries about
any priests you suspect of having gay leanings or ac-
tivities, unless it involves children.
4. You are to cease aggressively speaking against
gay marriage. A quiet demeanor is best.
Follow these instructions and your secret life
will be safe. Violate them and you will have a great
deal to explain. There are many more files like the
ones on the memory stick."

He addressed the envelop to the Archbishop
and marked it, *"Strictly Personal and Confidential."*

Al smiled. "This is a good deed I'm doing," he thought
to himself, "I need to reward myself. A weekend away maybe,
with Jake!"
He went to bed and tried to sleep, which was difficult.

Every time he dozed off, his legs would suddenly jump fitfully and awaken him. He promised himself a full day of rest to prepare for his little reward trip.

24

Billy had no idea where to go or
what to do after his phone call with Al. The thought of going
back to the rectory and explaining why he was suspended to
his pastor, Father Red Reilly, was daunting at best. He had a
great deal of respect for the old time Irish American priest, a
dying breed of tough, no nonsense men whose lives were dedicated to serving their community and the Church along with
a vibrant belief in the value of sports, party time and family.
The fact that Red was a recovering alcoholic gave Billy hope
that he wouldn't be too judgmental of his behavior but there
had never been any talk or hint of homosexuality in any of
their conversations and he wasn't sure exactly how homophobic Red might be.

His fears drove him to seek the safety of Sister Jane and
the recovery house, but he thought he needed to face the music at the rectory first, find out where he stood with the pastor

and then figure out what he would do next with his life.

As he opened the front door to the rectory, he was met by Mrs. Garcia, the housekeeper. "Oh Padre Billy, Father Red said he wanted to see you as soon as you came in. He is in his room."

"Gracias, Senora. Ya me voy ahorita," he replied.

Billy went to his room, took his coat off, lay it on the bed and dropped to his knees. He prayed for help and guidance, asking God to help him say the right thing at the right time. He got up, walked down the hall and gently knocked on the Pastor's door. The door flew open and Red reached out to gave Billy a big hug.

"Oh Billy, come in and tell me what the hell is going on. Are you all right? What did they do to you?" Red exclaimed. He directed Billy to the couch and sat next to him.

Billy was taken aback by the warmth of his reception given that he anticipated a rough interrogation.

"So, what did Father Cody tell you?"

"Nothing, except that you were suspended and that the AB was deciding your future over the next few days. He said you were to perform no priestly duties, but that it was not to be announced to the parish but kept confidential," Red replied.

"OK. Well, I don't know what to say."

"Tell me what you can. Maybe I can help you."

"The Archbishop has received an anonymous letter accusing me of having an affair and breaking up a good Catholic family."

"Is that all?"

"Well, first of all, I admitted it. But also that the affair is with the husband, not the wife," Billy said carefully watching Red's response.

"I see. That wouldn't be the first time that's ever been the case. I still don't see why that merits a suspension. I mean my God, if every priest who fell down on his vow of celibacy were suspended, there wouldn't be Masses in half the parishes. This seems a little extreme to me. If I were a guessing man, I would say the old man is jealous!" Red said with a laugh.

Billy laughed nervously.

"You're sure there's nothing else? Nothing with kids? No stealing?" Red asked with a wince.

"No. I think I disappointed the Archbishop. He doesn't like gay people, especially in the Church. He's had me spying on Sister Jane over at the recovery house because he thinks she might be a lesbian."

"That's nuts. Listen, just relax. I'm sure this really has you upset, but the punishment does not fit the crime here. I'm sure he's just trying to scare you and teach you a lesson. I'll go down to the AB's office tomorrow and plead your case. I should have been consulted in the first place. We'll get this suspension lifted right away. This whole matter should be in handled in the confessional, not in the Chancery office."

"Thank you, Father."

Red sat back on the couch and looked at a Billy. "Do you love him?"

"Yes I do, but it's over for me. He is happily married and has no intention of ending his marriage. He even told his wife and I've decided I must move on."

"Sometimes Billy these things may actually make you a better priest, give you more empathy and understanding of what people go through. Mind you I'm not recommending it, just that there are benefits from experiences, even the most painful and sinful ones. You have to trust that God is guiding you, all the time, all the way." Red gave Billy an encouraging smile.

"I suppose so. But I just don't know what to make about all this. I've been wondering if I should be a priest, if I can even be celibate, or if I even want to. I'm pretty confused," Billy said, looking back with sadness.

"And hurt I'm sure. Love always hurts. Plus the Church knows how to hurt us, maybe because we love her too. This is a good time to pray and search your heart. You have a real gift. You must know that everyone here loves you. I mean you have had such a positive effect on the whole parish. The Latino community in particular has fallen completely in love with you. They are touched by your sermons and your kind-nesses. I hear it all the time. God has touched you, Billy, I can tell. You have a great deal of love inside you to share, but I know from my own experience that the path is rarely straight and never clear."

"Thank you so much for your understanding and sup-port. I wasn't sure how you'd take to all this. I couldn't ask for a better pastor. I am so grateful." Billy got up.

"I'm here for you whenever you need me. Take good care of yourself. You need to be real good to Billy. He's spe-cial." Red stood and gave him another hug.

"So, I can stay here for a bit while I figure out what I'm going to do next?"

"Of course you can. We'll keep this between us until you hear something more definitive from 'his nibs'. There's something really strange about that man. He's as cold as an ice cube and constantly overreacts to anything sexual. But I saw how he looked at you when he was here for a visitation. It felt very possessive somehow, I don't know. There's something crooked there, I mean in his head. Do you mind if I go down tomorrow and talk with him about you? I mean, I am your pastor," Red asked.

"All right. I guess I need all the help I can get."

"Good. Now, we'll have a nice dinner tonight and talk of other things. I'd like to know more about Sister Jane's work myself. She sounds like a wonder."

"OK. I think I'm going to head down there myself. I need to talk with her about all this. She's been sort of a spiritual guide to me. I'll be back for dinner. Thank you so much for your support. I can't tell you how much it means to me." Billy smiled and received one last hug.

"God speed. Everything will be fine. Don't worry."

Billy went back to his room, took off his clerical shirt and black pants, put on jeans and a purple T-shirt and slipped out the back door of the rectory. He decided to walk through the Mission to the recovery house.

He felt a strange relief and a certain joy as he walked through the noise of the traffic, the smells of the flower bins in front of Bi-Rite market, the bright colors of the outdoor vegetable and fruit stalls and the vague scent of chorizo from the numerous Taquerias along 16th Street. He had grown to really love this neighborhood and feel like he belonged, not as a priest but as one of the many thousands of Latino immigrants who risked everything to come to the U.S. and make this place their new home. He thought of his first memories of the Mission when he arrived at the age of thirteen, unable to speak a word of English, a bit overwhelmed by the traffic and bigness of nearly everything in America. He had felt at home in the streets where Spanish was heard more often than English and the smells were of the Mexico he had left behind. As he walked today, he noticed no one paid attention to him, no one stared, no one acknowledged him in any way, at least not the way people did when he wore his priestly shirt.

Arriving at the recovery house, the crowds were already gathering for the daily Vespers service. He joined in and found a seat near the back. As the service began, he sang the familiar songs, recited the age-old prayers and knelt for the blessing just as everyone else. He was one among the many who needed healing. He was no one special and he liked that feeling. He liked too that his secrets were somehow out to the world. The Archbishop, his pastor, his lover's wife. They all knew about him, that he was gay, that he needed love, that he was a sexual person who wanted to give love and express it and that he was a very human man. There was healing in these thoughts and a feeling of acceptance. It wasn't another's acceptance of him, after all, the Archbishop certainly did not accept him, but his acceptance was of himself. There was a relief that he didn't need to hide anymore. As he was suspended, he didn't need to play a role either. He could be just Billy Fernandez in a way he never felt he could before. Kneeling as the service ended, he said a prayer of gratitude. He reflected that with everything going on in his life over the past week, he was surprised that he was thankful. He actually believed God was working in his life and that he was exactly where he was supposed to be.

He went looking for Sister Jane but could not find her with the throng that was leaving the Church. He headed toward her residence at the back of the center and found her sitting on the stairs leading up to her room.

"Are you all right?"

"Oh hello, Billy. Yes, I think so. I'm just exhausted and don't have the energy to climb the stairs right now. Come sit," she replied with a weary smile. She moved to the side to make room for him. "I just don't know how much longer I can do this. I mean, there are more and more people every day. It just takes so much out of me. Plus Sister Gertrude has gone back to Philadelphia, so I'm running the place by myself. But enough of me, what's up with you?"

"I've been suspended," Billy replied casually.

"What? What for? Is it because of this place?"

"No, although the Archbishop didn't much like my report about you. There wasn't anything negative in it, and he was really looking for something damning. No, someone wrote a letter to him outing me and accusing me of breaking up a good Catholic family, so he knows all about John and me. He hasn't quite decided what to do with me."

"Oh, I'm so sorry Billy, that must hurt a great deal," she said, putting an arm around his shoulder.

"Thank you. It's funny, but it has sort of liberated me to do some serious thinking about my life and what I want. I think I really am confused. The only place I feel at peace is during your Vespers service and being at this place."

"Well, I'm glad to hear that. I could certainly use some help if you want to come around more often," Jane said, smiling at Billy.

"Really? I don't know what the Archbishop is going to do. Maybe send me to some distant parish or a monastery or some center where they fix gay priests. I don't really care. I think I want to take a leave of absence and figure things out. I know Father Red would be glad for me to stay at Mission Dolores. He's been just so wonderful about all this, but if you have a spare room I'd rather stay here. I'd be glad to do whatever you need done."

"That would be a big help to me! I would love it, but I think you should think it over for a day or so and talk with Father Red. You should also wait until you hear from the Archbishop," Jane offered. She gave him a nudge of her shoulder.

"Staying here won't help your reputation much, but I guess you're over that now."

"I'm afraid it's your reputation that may be damaged now, not mine," Billy replied with a chuckle.

"I guess neither one of us cares much anymore. We are both outcasts just doing the Lord's work. Let the high and mighty do what they will."

25

Al's phone pinged that he had a new text message. He was surprised that it was from Father Bob Cody. "No worries, he's decided to back off, even on your boy and that nun.'

Al smiled. Mission accomplished. He felt proud of himself. Another escape from danger and nothing linked to him in any way. Just like in the old days. Plus, he had done a good deed for Billy and Sister what's-her-name.

He texted Jake, "Hey. Feeling like a little celebration. Want to join me for a long weekend in Vegas? First class all the way."

He smiled at himself, a smile of self-satisfaction. He even giggled a little. It was the best he had felt in a long time.

Al waited for a reply but nothing came back. His exhilaration and anticipation quickly turned to anger and jealousy as Jake's lack of response could only mean he was fucking another guy at that moment. He grew more agitated with every passing minute. He started to pace the floor of his room. "Fuck him," he muttered to himself.

Al walked over to his computer and waited impatiently as it booted, then opened the rentaboy.com web page. He searched through the profiles looking for a likely candidate to take to Las Vegas. It took a while to sort through the 200 plus profiles, but it kept his mind off Jake and the jealous feelings that were raging through his head.

He was down to three finalists when his phone pinged a text message: "Vegas sounds fun. Can leave tonight but have to be back Mon."

Al's mood changed immediately. He wanted to go with Jake, someone he had grown to trust, who knew how to soothe him and nurture him. Plus, he was a guaranteed fun time in bed. "Great. I'll make reservations and get back to you. What name for your ticket should I use?"

"Cloud Daniels."

Al set about getting flights and booking a suite at the Venetian. His calendar showed he was supposed to say Mass on Sunday at the Cathedral so he emailed the secretary that he had been called out of town unexpectedly and another priest needed to be found. He looked up shows in Las Vegas and decided to book a Friday night performance of Cirque du Soleil. His excitement grew as he made plans for the weekend. It would be a fun, raucous and wild time with a very cute boy, surrounded by glitter and luxury. No one would know him nor pay attention to them. Las Vegas offered just the right level of anonymity: total.

He picked Jake up in a stretch limo for the trip to the airport.

"Well, this is my first limo ride. Very comfy," Jake said

stretching out and laying his head back on the smooth leather. "Sweet!"

"It's going to be first class all the way. I'm in a party mood," Al replied.

"Fun! Can I ask why?"

"Oh, your friend Emily proved to be invaluable in helping me put a cork into some nasty business by my boss. I'm as safe as can be now and I even helped some other folks in the process. It was a masterfully executed political move. I feel like I have my old stuff back and I just want to celebrate. I couldn't think of anybody I'd rather do that with than you," Al reached over and gave Jake a peck on the lips. Jake responded with a full deep kiss.

"Vegas, here we come!"

They checked into the Venetian hotel, unpacked, showered and got dressed for the evening. Al had only been able to get tickets to the early performance of Cirque du Soleil, which started at six, so they agreed to have dinner afterward. Al popped a bottle of champagne from the mini bar as they dressed. He watched admiringly as Jake put on a pinkish purple shirt that seemed to shine with sequins though there weren't any sequins to be seen. Tight black pants and a light blue coat finished the outfit. His clothes fit his firm muscular body.

"What do you think?" Jake asked as he twirled around.

"You look so hot. I could eat you up right now!" Al replied.

"Don't you worry. I'll be your dessert!"

Finishing their champagne with a few kisses, it was time to head out to the theatre.

Six hours later, Jake and Al staggered back through their room door. Falling on the bed, Al let out a moan.

"I am so full," he sighed.

"I can't believe you ate that whole piece of prime rib. You do love your red meat!" Jake said in jest but with a slight critical note.

"Ahhgh! Well, there was more wine, so I had to keep eating. Besides, it was delicious." Al sat up. "Time for a little cognac. For digestive purposes, of course! Look in the mini bar and see if you can find a couple of mini-bottles." Al was slurring his words slightly and waved in the direction of the built-in refrigerator.

Jake dutifully complied and finding a couple of small bottles, opened them and handed one to Al.

"Cheers!" Al said, toasting Jake. Then drank the entire bottle down. "Ooouff, I feel better already. Say, you are over-dressed. You are cute as shit, but I love you naked more."

Jake took a sip, laughed and began to undress. "Are you sure you're up for this? You've had a lot to eat and drink."

"I've been dreaming of you all night. Of course, I'm up for you!" Al exclaimed, as he began to rip his clothes off.

They rolled around in bed playfully, kissing and licking each other with an occasional slap on the butt cheek. Al sucked Jake for a while, getting him hard and ready.

"Whatcha want to do?" Jake asked.

"Oh, I want you to fuck me good, but first give me a couple of those magic little pills you always have."

Jake reached over to his pants lying on the floor and took out a couple of blue pills and handed them to Al, "You sure?"

"Oh yeah, I love the way I feel with this stuff," he replied.

Al took the pills, swallowed them with the remains of Jake's cognac. He then continued to kiss, suck and lick Jake with delight. "I want to ride this lovely cock. Lay down," Al commanded.

Al climbed on top of him and began to moan as Jake fucked him.

"Yes, yes. Don't stop," Al pleaded, with a raspy growl in his throat. As they continued their lovemaking, as his ecstasy soared, it became harder and harder for Al to breathe. He coughed once, then twice and then Al pitched forward onto Jake. For Al, suddenly, everything went dark.

Al looked down from the ceiling. It was utterly quiet, yet he could see Jake yelling and pounding on his chest. Jake tried to blow air into Al's lungs. He then wildly grabbed the phone on the nightstand and called for help.

"Goodbye Jake. I'm going now. I don't want to come back."

Al twisted away from the scene below and gravitated toward the warmth, an all-embracing white light that was lovingly pulling him out of the room. He gazed back at his lifeless body on the bed. He was suddenly frightened and pained by the many hurts he had endured and the ones that he had inflicted on others. These flashed before him. He wanted to cry out, but he could not.

Al surrendered to the immense love that was drawing him away. This was what he had wanted, all along.

Dennis Paul Stradford is a retired business executive currently devoting his time to writing, community service and supporting emerging technology companies.

Redeemed and Enlightened is the third novel of a trilogy that began with *Blessed and Betrayed* and *Betrayed and Redeemed* published in 2011 and 2013 respectively.

Prior to a 36 year career with both public and private high tech companies, he studied to be a Roman Catholic priest. He holds a B.A. in history from San Jose State University and an M.A. and M.Div. from St. Patrick's University.

239

SANCTUS SPIRITUS
PRESS

San Francisco